√√01

P- 95

DATE DUE			
APR 4 01	⊍		
JY 12 01			
NO 2 02			
JA 02 03			
10-15-19			

3/01

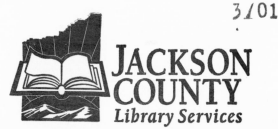

JACKSON COUNTY
Library Services

HEADQUARTERS
413 West Main Street
Medford, Oregon 97501

WILEY'S MOVE

G·K
Hall
&Co.

Also by Lee Hoffman
in Large Print:

Bred to Kill
The Valdez Horses

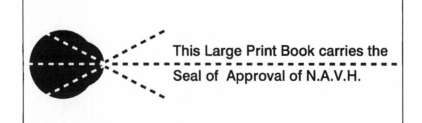

This Large Print Book carries the
Seal of Approval of N.A.V.H.

WILEY'S MOVE

LEE HOFFMAN

G.K. Hall & Co. • Thorndike, Maine

Published in 2001 by arrangement with Golden West Literary Agency.

G.K. Hall Large Print Western Series.

The text of this Large Print edition is unabridged.
Other aspects of the book may vary from the original edition.

Set in 16 pt. Plantin by Rick Gundberg.

Printed in the United States on permanent paper.

Library of Congress Cataloging-in-Publication Data

Hoffman, Lee, 1932–
  Wiley's move / Lee Hoffman.
    p. cm.
  ISBN 0-7838-9355-8 (lg. print : hc : alk. paper)
  1. Texas — Fiction. 2. Large type books. I. Title.
  PS3558.O346 W55 2001
   813′.54—dc21   00-053849

To Mom and Dad.

CHAPTER 1

Hardly, Texas, wasn't much. Nothing at all like it had set out to be back when Big Jim Boohm, the one folks called the Builder, founded it.

When the Union Pacific and Central Pacific linked rails at Promontory Point in Utah, Big Jim Boohm had decided the next transcontinental railway would likely run up and down the nation from Mexico to Canada. He platted Hardly, figuring it was a natural place for a division point when the railroad came through. Then he moved on to start a new town in Guatemala, where he felt certain someone was bound to dig a canal across the isthmus before long.

As yet, the only public carrier into Hardly was a stagecoach that arrived from the county seat once a month, then turned around and went back a day or two later. This service was the result of an error in a clerk's transcription of the terms of franchise whereby the coach line held an otherwise lucrative monopoly. So, whether it carried passengers or not, whether it carried cargo or not, the monthly coach to Hardly ran with remarkable regularity.

Alongside the lonely road that stretched across the *llano* toward town, three men hunkered in the shade of their horses, waiting. A shadow skimmed close to them. One man looked up. He frowned as he recognized the bird for a vulture. Buzzards could be bad omens.

The coach was cutting along the road like a plow, casting up a high furrow of dust. The curtains were drawn and buttoned, but the dust filtered through to spread itself over the travel-weary passengers.

The two women were sitting side by side, facing forward. The lone man sat opposite them, riding backwards, feeling a little nauseated.

Like the coach, Weston Finlay was on his way to Hardly because of a mistake. A half-deaf ticket agent had interpreted an introduction, "Weston Finlay," as a destination, "West of Hardly." Failing to catch the words that followed, he had directed the passenger to the coach that was, at that very moment, readying to leave. Weston had hurriedly ensconced himself inside.

He had not yet learned of his error. He sat with one hand pressed gently against his stomach, wondering how much farther to the next stop, and how much longer to his ultimate destination, the town of Bitter Drip, Arizona.

The woman across from him, by far the older of the two, was talking. Her voice blended with the rattle of the coach, providing a somewhat unwelcome accompaniment to his thoughts. He hoped he wasn't going to be ill.

He suddenly realized that she had asked him a question.

"I do beg your pardon, Mrs. Quick," he said, mildly pleased that he had recalled her name. In the days when he had been a drummer for Slattery's Superior Specialties, his two major problems had been a tendency to motion sickness and an inability to remember names.

She repeated, "I believe you mentioned that you are a widower."

"Yes. My dear wife passed on only last year." He sighed appropriately.

"The late Colonel Quick met his demise in the war," Mrs. Quick said. "For the Confederacy, you know. He was of fine old Southern stock. As the eldest son, he had inherited the estates."

"Mrs. Finlay was the former Felicity Slattery," Weston said. "The only child of J. J. Slattery. Slattery's Superior Specialties. You've heard of J. J. Slattery, of course?"

She gave a curt nod and continued. "It was most tragic. My husband gone, and the estates all destroyed. All seemed lost. It is extremely difficult for a woman of my breeding to be alone and comfortless in the world, you know."

"He formulated the famous Old Doc Slattery's Superior Soothing Syrup," Weston said. "Undoubtedly the finest soothing syrup on the market."

"I actually had to take employment," Mrs. Quick went on. "With a most genteel family, of course. As governess to their daughter. A charming, thoroughly well-bred child."

"Unfortunately, some illnesses are beyond the

9

curative powers of even the most marvelous advances of modern science." Weston pressed his hand harder against his stomach and gave a small cough. "A man cursed from birth with weakness of constitution has small hope of ever enjoying the full robust health he longs for. However, I understand that the warm, dry climate and the mineral waters of Bitter Drip are almost miraculous. Have you ever been to Bitter Drip before, Mrs. Quick?"

"Bitter Drip?" She shook her head thoughtfully. "I can't say I've even heard of it."

His brows rose in surprise. "But aren't you going there?"

"No. We're going to the town of Hardly." She gestured toward the girl at her side. "Miss Lucinda, here, is to be married there. To Mr. Hash Harker. Perhaps you've heard of him?"

"No, I'm afraid not," he said. "I suppose Hardly is a waystop."

"I was given to understand that it is the end of the line."

"What?"

"Yes, I'm certain of it. Someone at the ticket office mentioned it. Hardly is the end of this run."

Weston Finlay darted a pleading look toward the younger woman. He hoped she would say Mrs. Quick was in error. But Miss Lucinda Cummins of Fairwater, Virginia, sat gazing straight ahead, lost in her own thoughts. Weston swallowed hard. With anxious fingers, he unbut-

10

toned the window curtain closest to him and shouted out at the driver.

Whisk Shaker had driven this run often. He'd been driving one thing or another since he was a pup, some forty-odd years ago. His hands held the reins, knowing them, knowing every small tug from the team, without a thought from his mind. His head was filled entirely with red and black, circles and squares.

It was Deke Wiley's move. It had been for two days before Deke packed off to Mexico on business. The checkerboard with the game in progress sat on an upended keg at the coach-line stable in Hardly, waiting.

Whisk hoped that Deke would be back and make a play before it came time to roll the coach out again. All month he'd been studying the game. He had lost the last six games to Deke. He felt if he lost this one, too, it would kill his spirit. So he had studied and planned every play he could imagine, and he'd thought up a counter-move for each one. He figured he had Deke licked for sure this time.

He heard the hollering from within the coach. That passenger with the derby seemed to be calling him. He ignored the first call, pretending he couldn't hear over the noise of the coach and team. He reckoned the little man wanted to stop and run off into the bushes somewhere. But there weren't any bushes around here big enough for a man to hide behind, and Hardly wasn't much farther ahead.

11

Weston Finlay kept shouting.

Finally Whisk shouted back, "Hold your water. We'll be into town right soon."

"You've *got* to stop!" Weston insisted at the top of his voice.

If it was that desperate, Whisk decided, he'd better let the little feller get out and piss. He leaned back on the reins. The horses eased their pace. Whisk applied his boot to the brake lever. Squealing, the coach rolled to a stop.

"All right, make it quick," Whisk hollered. He didn't want to mess around out here. He wanted to get on into town and see if Deke Wiley had made his move yet. Speak of the devil, there were Deke's three boys riding up out of a hollow just ahead. He couldn't mistake those long bony bastards at any distance.

The coach door swung open, and Weston Finlay came bounding anxiously out. Running to the nigh-front wheel, he craned his neck and looked up at the driver.

"I've got to talk to you!"

"Talk," Whisk grumbled, his eyes on the riders galloping toward him.

"Does this stage go to Bitter Drip in Arizona Territory?" Weston asked.

"No."

"Where does it go?"

"Nowhere, if you don't get back on board so's I can start it moving again."

"But . . ." Weston began.

Whisk waved sociably at the riders.

12

". . . I'm going to Bitter Drip."

"Not on this coach, you ain't."

They waved back.

"But . . ." Weston said.

The riders came up on the nigh side.

"Howdy, boys," Whisk said as they reined in. From the bandannas they had over their faces, he reckoned they'd been riding dusty. Trailing a herd, maybe. He hoped they'd brought in the beef cattle that Deke went to Mexico for.

He asked them, "Your Pa with you?"

The man on the dun shook his head. He had his Colt revolver out of the holster. The hand with the gun rested against his thigh. Lifting it, he said, "Hold it, Whisk. Tie them lines and get your hands up."

Whisk ignored the order. Scowling, he said, "What you talking about, Jesse? What you boys up to?"

"How'd he know who we are?" the boy on the bald-faced bay squeaked. Jody was the youngest of the Wiley boys, and he had high hopes for this adventure. Masking their faces with bandannas had been his idea.

"Who else would we be but us?" Jess answered him.

Jacob, the oldest of the three, said, "I told you a mask wouldn't do me no good if I didn't cover my eyes. I got real special eyes. You ask any gal. I got the kind of eyes folks can't help but remember."

13

"I want to go to Bitter Drip," Weston Finlay said, his voice trailing off like a run-down Edison gramophone.

All three riders had their guns out now. All were pointing them toward Whisk. He surveyed them, worked his jaw, spat in the dust, and said, "What you think you're doing? Holding up this coach?"

"Kinda," Jess said.

"Of all the damned — You're gonna make me late," Whisk said. "Is your Pa back from Mexico yet?"

Jess shook his head. "Expecting word from him anytime now."

Weston looked from one to the other, not quite comprehending. He wondered if he could be having a nightmare.

"Come on," Jacob said. He stepped down off his horse and held the reins out to Jody. "Here, hold this."

"How's Mrs. Deke these days, Jesse?" Whisk asked.

"Fine."

"And your sisters?"

"Fine."

"All but that damn July," Jody put in. "That no-good little pest won't leave her hands off our guns. She up and swiped all the ammunition out of them this morning. If we hadn't been lucky enough to notice it, we'd all be out here now holding up this coach with empty guns."

14

"You planning on doing some shooting?" Whisk said.

"Hell, no," Jess answered.

The door of the coach was hanging open. Jacob walked over and looked in.

"One of you ladies Miss Lucinda Cummins of Fairwater, Virginia?" he said, pulling off his hat in a mannerly fashion.

"Don't you answer him, Cindy," Miss Delphinia Quick snapped.

The girl eyed Jacob and said, "I am."

He grinned. "Well, suppose you just step out here a minute, ma'am."

"No!" Mrs. Quick said. "Don't do it!"

"I don't mean to hurt you none," Jacob said in his best woman-courting voice.

The girl started to rise.

"Cindy!" Mrs. Quick sounded horrified.

"Just for a minute," Miss Lucinda said. "I'll be right back."

Her tiny pointy-toed boot emerged from the shadowed interior of the coach. Then a flouncy mass of ruffles. Holding her skirts up just enough to show the row of buttons on her boot, Miss Lucinda put her foot on the step iron.

Jacob held a hand out to her. As she accepted it, she smiled at him. Gracefully, she lowered herself from the coach.

Whisk watched with a darkening scowl. He didn't mind a little simple highway robbery now and then. Hell, he'd dabbled in it himself when he was younger. But he had strong objections to

15

a man being discourteous to womenfolk.

Jacob jerked down his bandanna, baring his grin.

A hint of a frown flickered across Miss Lucinda's face. She'd read a lot about highwaymen in those little paperbound books that one had to hide away from one's parents. During the whole long dull trip west, she'd been hoping for a holdup. But she'd expected the road agents to be more dashing. At the least, properly bathed and well-kempt. Jacob didn't fit the image at all.

Yet . . .

There was something about him. Something rugged and rough-hewn and very unlike the men she'd been acquainted with in Fairwater, Virginia.

Cautiously she asked, "What do you want with me?"

"Just to taste them sweet honey lips of yours before Hash Harker does," he said, slipping his revolver back into its holster. He reached both arms out toward her. "You're gonna like this."

Jody grinned under his mask. He sure admired his big brother. Envied him. Jacob was hell on wheels with the womenfolk.

"You stop that, Jacob Wiley!" Whisk hollered.

Jacob paid him no mind.

Whisk reached for the snub-nosed Greener he kept under the box.

"Hey!" Jess shouted as he realized where Whisk's hand was going.

Jody's thoughts were all on women until he

16

saw the barrel of the Greener. It looked like the muzzle of a Napoleon gun. Startled, he winced.

For an instant they were all surrounded by sudden thunder. Then the sound lost itself in the vastness of the *llano,* leaving a silence as loud as the blast had been.

The shotgun slid out of Whisk's hands. It clattered on the road. The hoofbeats of a running horse seemed to echo it.

Wide-eyed, Whisk said, "You've shot me. You've done went and shot me."

Jody looked down at the smoking Colt in his hand.

Jacob turned away from the girl to stare at the horse Jody'd been holding for him. It was racing off across the plain, reins and stirrups flapping.

"Oh, hell," Jess said.

CHAPTER 2

Miss Lucinda Cummins of Fairwater, Virginia, stared aghast at Jacob Wiley. Jacob gazed after his rapidly disappearing horse. Weston Finlay eyed Jody and the gun with shocked apprehension. Jody gaped at the smoking Colt in his own hand. Jess watched appalled as Whisk Shaker slowly slid out of sight in the well of the driver's seat.

Mrs. Delphinia Quick hefted herself down from the coach. Surveying the situation, she said, "You've killed him."

"You'll all hang!" Weston Finlay gasped.

Jody dropped his gun.

Jacob sucked a deep breath and ran. Flinging himself astride behind Jody, he drove his spurs at the horse's sides. Jody's rowels hit hide at the same moment. With an angry snort, the horse plunged into a gallop.

Jess's dun wanted to follow. It danced with frightened impatience as he held tight on the reins. On the edge of the driver's box, he saw fingers. They touched the brake lever. Crept slowly up it and gripped. Whisk Shaker's tousled white hair appeared, then his face. He grimaced at Jess.

"You hurt bad?" Jess asked him.

He got himself onto his feet. Clutching his left arm, he said with pride, "Hell, no. He only just barely nicked me."

"Need help?"

"You'll all hang!" Weston Finlay said again.

Whisk said, "Jesse, you know that kid brother of yours just up and shot me?"

Jess nodded. "I don't think he meant to do it."

"No. Don't reckon so," Whisk agreed. "Boy, I got a notion maybe you better light."

"I reckon," Jess said. He looked around at Miss Lucinda Cummins of Fairwater, Virginia. She was still standing by the open door of the coach, but now it was Jess she stared at.

He jerked the bandanna away from his face and nudged his mount toward her. She didn't move. He couldn't tell whether she was boldly standing her ground or scared too stiff to run. He sidled the horse up to her.

The huge woman who'd been last to come out of the coach stepped to the girl's side. Her large round face was topped with a hatful of lavender-dyed egret plumes. They quivered as she shook a fist at him. "You stay away from her!"

"Dunno if this'll count or not," Jess muttered to himself. He leaned out of the saddle, caught Miss Lucinda by the shoulder, and pulled her toward him.

"Stop that!" the woman under the lavender plumes bellowed.

"Jesse Wiley!" Whisk hollered indignantly.

Miss Lucinda's wide soft eyes held to Jess's

19

face. Her small pink mouth formed an uncertain circle.

Roughly, quickly, he kissed her.

"I'll have the Rangers on you for this!" Mrs. Delphinia Quick bellowed.

Jess backed the dun a step. Miss Lucinda was motionless. Her eyes were closed. She opened them enough to peek out at him from under her lashes. He touched the brim of his hat to her, then wheeled the dun and set his spurs to it.

He was maybe a dozen long strides away when he heard the pop. It sounded like one of the little garter guns some women were so fond of carrying.

He heard Whisk Shaker shout, "Stop that!"

He expected it was the lavender-plumed woman who'd shot at him. Glancing back, he saw the glint of sunlight on a nickel-plated pistol. To his surprise, it was in the hands of the man in the derby. In both of his hands, held straight out as if he were afraid of it. It popped again, making a monstrous puff of smoke for a weapon so small.

Jess waved.

Whisk waved back at him.

So did Miss Lucinda Cummins of Fairwater, Virginia.

Jody's mount was a bald-faced bay with a full barrel, sturdy legs, and just a little white showing at the eye. It had the bottom for long hard work, but it had a lazy streak as well. It didn't hanker to gallop far carrying double. Tentatively, it slowed. It got a jab of spurs in response. With a disgusted snort, it pushed into a gallop again.

Jody's first panic eventually faded into thought. When the bay tried slowing again, he failed to react. He was paying no attention now to where the horse was headed or how fast it was traveling. Once the bay was certain of this, it settled into a walk and started hunting graze.

Jacob didn't notice either. Like his kid brother, he'd gone from startled fear to deep thought. Under his breath he mumbled, "Poor old Whisk."

Jody heard the soft words close behind his ear. He nodded and said, "Jacob, I really done wrong, didn't I?"

"You sure as hell did."

"I'm sorry." The boy wondered if his brother could ever forgive him. He sure hoped so. There was nobody in the whole world he admired as much as Jacob.

Thinly he said, "Likely I'm a real disappointment to you?"

Jacob almost answered yes, but something in Jody's tone stopped him. After a moment he said, "I don't reckon you meant for it to go the way it did."

"I sure didn't!"

"And it's done and over, so there's no changing it."

"Uh-huh."

They rode in silence for a few moments more. Then Jody asked, "What we gonna do now?"

"Now?" Jacob glanced back over his shoulder, searching the horizon behind him. "Funny that Jesse ain't caught up with us yet."

Jody hadn't noticed. Taken aback, he said, "You don't reckon nothing's happened to him?"

"Hell, no! Ain't nothing never gonna happen to Jesse. Maybe he didn't come after us. Maybe he took off in a different direction."

"He wouldn't do that, would he? He wouldn't leave us alone?"

"He'll be along," Jacob insisted. He looked back again. The horizon was still empty. "Boy, you ain't got a bottle on you nowhere, have you?"

"No."

"What you say we ride on into town, stop by Dominic's, and pick us up one?"

"Town? Jacob, I just killed poor old Whisk. Folks in town ain't likely to take too kindly to that."

"That's true. Look, we could go on home. I got me a bottle hid there."

"Pa ain't likely to take too kindly to it either. Him and Whisk was awful good friends."

"You reckon Pa's back home by now?"

"I don't know."

Jacob made a thoughtful sound in his throat. He sure didn't look forward to hearing what Deke Wiley was going to say about all this.

"Maybe we ought to hole up awhile and think on it," he suggested.

Jody nodded agreement. "Where?"

22

"I sure wish Jesse was here," Jacob mumbled.

"Where you reckon we ought to hole up?"

"Hell, I don't know. Look, we got to get together with Jesse. We can't up and leave him to face this all by himself."

"Maybe we ought to go out to Coyote Gulch," Jody said. "He'd know that's where we went, wouldn't he?"

"Sure! We've hid out there from Pa plenty enough times when we was all kids. It's just the place!"

Jody kicked the bay into a lope. He had a destination now, and for a while his thoughts were all involved with getting there. But then he began to think as how the gulch would only be a stopping place.

"We'll have to go on somewhere from there," he said aloud.

"Huh?"

"There's likely to be real trouble, ain't there, Jacob? I mean, with the law, maybe. Coach people, they ain't gonna like it that I killed Whisk. They'll send in the sheriff or the Rangers or something. And folks in town, maybe they'll get up to lynch us. That could happen, couldn't it? We're gonna have to go away from here, ain't we?"

"Leave home?"

"Uh-huh."

Jacob considered. "I reckon so."

"You think maybe January'd come with us?"

"Hell, we can't go asking her to come along on

23

the owlhoot trail with us."

"We gonna be outlaws, Jacob?"

"Reckon we're gonna have to. What else we gonna do? Go get us cow work for thirty and found? Go live in Mexico like the Indians? I wasn't cut out for no life like that."

Jody nodded.

"I'm a big man," Jacob went on, warming to his subject. "I'm meant for high living. Lots of good liquor and women and fast horses and stuff. If I got to be a outlaw, I'm gonna be one like the Renos or them Jameses and Youngers."

"The James Brothers? Yeah, Jacob! You and me and Jesse. We could be the Wiley Brothers. We could sure show all them owlhoots, couldn't we?"

"We sure could."

"When we gonna start?"

"Right soon. Only . . ." Jacob hesitated. "Only we can't just up and go off. We got to pay our respects to poor old Whisk."

"What you mean?"

"We got to see him proper into the ground."

"You mean we're going to the burying?"

"Don't you want to? Whisk was our friend, boy. It's our bounden duty. Rightly, us and Pa ought to be the pallbearers."

"Us?"

"Who else? Who was any better friends to Whisk than us? Jody, that old man was like a second Pa to me. When I was just a little tad, I used to hang around the coach stable, and he'd let me help him shovel manure and clean the harness and sometimes I'd meet him out on the road and ride into town on the box with him and he'd learn me about driving a team, and he used to say when he got around to going trapping up to the Canady woods, he'd take me along and we'd make us our fortune in pelts, like the old-timey mountain men used to do."

Overwhelmed by his own words, Jacob paused.

Jody blinked and snuffled and said, "He done all kinda things like that for me, too, when I was little."

"Uh-huh."

"He was a awful good old man, Jacob. And I've went and killed him."

"Uh-huh."

"Least I can do now is pay my respects to him, ain't it?"

"Damn right! It wouldn't be decent if we didn't."

"Only . . . only, if we show up at the burying, folks might take a mind to lynch us."

"That's so."

Studying the problem, Jody let the bay slow to a walk again.

Jacob glanced back over his shoulder and muttered, "I sure wish Jesse'd catch up with us."

"Maybe we could wear disguises," Jody suggested.

"Huh?"

"Like play-actors. You know. Put on wigs and

whiskers and lumpy noses."

"Maybe . . . No, wouldn't do me no good, boy. They'd know me by my eyes. I got the kind of eyes can't nobody forget once he's looked into them."

"Uh-huh." Jody was sorely disappointed. It had seemed like a good suggestion when he thought of it.

"Well," Jacob said. "We *got* to be there. Ain't no way around that. It's our bounden duty to old Whisk. I reckon we'll just have to take our chances."

"I sure wish Jesse was here," Jody said. "He comes up with good ideas."

"Look, we'll hole up in the gulch, give him time to find us. If he ain't showed by sundown, we can ride into town kinda quiet like and see Junie. If there's anything happened we should know about, her and Dominic will have heard by then."

Jody nodded and spurred the bay back into a lope.

"I sure wish you had the habit of carrying a bottle," Jacob mumbled.

Jess had been following Jacob and Jody, but before he got within sight of them, he halted and sat back thoughtfully.

He reckoned he ought to go ahead and catch up with his brothers. After all, they were all Wileys, and they had to stick together. But something in him sure hankered to cut off in some other direction and just keep going. Sometimes he got downright tired of always backing up his brothers when they got into trouble. Seemed like he was always so busy backing them that he never had the time to get into any good trouble of his own.

He was still sitting there when the shadow of a bird flashed past him. He blinked and frowned up at the black speck against the sky. He thought it was the same damn buzzard he'd seen earlier. Again, he wondered if it was an omen.

The buzzard seemed to be heading straight toward the Wiley place. Sighing, Jess lifted rein and set off in the same direction.

CHAPTER 3

The vulture passed over the Wiley place, swung
back, and came to rest in the high branches of a
pecan tree. The tree was the larger and scragglier
of a pair planted near a natural seep hole. They
yielded a few thick-husked, hard-shelled knots of
nuts every season. But Mrs. Deke Wiley didn't
care about the nuts. With no teeth left, she had
small interest in such things. She liked the trees
themselves. They stirred recollections for her.
Deke Wiley'd had the saplings brought in as a gift
for her when she was carrying Jacob, her firstborn.
He'd planted them for her with his own hands.

Sitting in the rocker on the back porch, Mrs.
Deke recollected how her man had been in those
days. A fine man, Deke Wiley. He'd done all the
planning of the house and the kitchen and the
other outbuildings, and some of the work of
putting them up, too. He'd had to finish off the
roofing himself after that half-breed Hopi they'd
rescued from the mission at San-Something-or-
Other ran away. They'd never been able to get
hold of another handyman like that 'breed, and
somehow Mr. Wiley never got around to paint-
ing the place or putting the door on the backhouse. But it didn't matter. Not to Mrs. Deke.

She sat with her bottle of laudanum in her lap and rocked fro and to, basking in the pleasure of her life.

The Wiley house had been built four-square, a room in each corner and a porch on each end. It sat up off the ground on naked stilts of piled-up rocks. Breezes under the house kept it cooler, and there was plenty of shade under there for the hounds.

The kitchen was separate, set a way back from the house, so that the heat of cooking wouldn't warm up the whole place. Deke figured on covering over the space between the two buildings with a dogtrot one of these days. He would have done it by now if that damned ungrateful Indian he'd given food and shelter of a sort hadn't up and took off, and it was hard for a man to get building work done without a little help. It had never occurred to Deke to put his sons to the job.

The outbuildings, like the house and kitchen, had never been painted. The unseasoned planks Deke had got in trade for some half-broke horses he'd traded from a couple of Mexicans for a cap-and-ball rifle had shrunk and warped until the walls had the look of rail fences. But, as Deke pointed out, it let the air blow through, which was a fine thing in such warm country. Mrs. Deke had commented a time or two about how it let a lot of dirt in, too. But after her first daughter, January, got old enough to help with the housework, she didn't mention it anymore.

January would mention it occasionally to her twin brother, Jess. She had nagged him about it so much that he'd finally up and chinked a few of the worst cracks with mud from the seep hole. That helped some. Not much.

Like the pecan trees, the iron range in the kitchen had been a special present to Mrs. Deke from her man. He'd traded a good Mexican bull for it. He'd never said where he got the bull.

Mrs. Deke had passed the range along to January on the girl's thirteenth birthday. From then on, the kitchen had been January's. So had the wash tubs and the broom. Mrs. Deke, having brought a fine healthy girl-child to age, sat back in her rocker, sipped her laudanum, and contemplated the goodness of her life.

January was the oldest girl, but not the only one. She and Jess had been followed by Junie. And after Jody, there was July, the youngest of the bunch.

Mrs. Deke had figured that once January went to wife, Junie could take over the kitchen, and when she was gone, it'd be July's turn. None of it worked out quite that way, though. Junie had up and moved into town over a year ago, and July couldn't be kept near housework, even at gunpoint. But January had discouraged her gentlemen callers until they all gave up coming around. Now she was in her twenties, well past her prime, and still at home, with no prospects.

It sorrowed Mrs. Deke that the girl didn't have herself a man, but she reckoned January would be a comfort to her and Mr. Wiley in their declining years.

Where was Mr. Wiley anyway, she wondered. He'd been gone off to Mexico for days now. She sure was looking forward to seeing him again.

Her musing drifted into soft memories and vague dreams. Suddenly she started. She thought she had glimpsed Mr. Wiley up there in the high branches of the pecan tree.

She had an impression of him all decked out in black, squatting on a limb. She wished he'd come on down. For one thing, there was a present waiting for him.

Junie had sent a fat German sausage in from town for her Pa. It was hanging on a porch post now, ripening in the sun. Mrs. Deke wondered if maybe it shouldn't be moved to a shadier place before it got too ripe. Maybe it ought to have a cloth draped over it to keep the flies away. But, on the other hand, if Mr. Wiley was back now, he'd eat it before it ripened anymore, and he could wipe the flyspecks off first if he wanted to, so there was nothing to worry about.

She wondered why he didn't come on down from the tree. He sure must know she was waiting for him.

Her eyelids fluttered, then were still over the flickering images in her mind. She held her laudanum bottle in her lap as she creaked back and forth in the rocker. January sat on the floor with her bare feet dangling while she shelled corn into a bowl in her lap. Occasionally she flicked a kernel to the chickens that clustered at her feet. They flapped and squawked in their eagerness to get the tidbits. She paid them no attention. Her thoughts were far away. So far that she didn't even notice the clop of hooves in the yard.

From under drooping lashes, Mrs. Deke watched her middle son, Jess, ride over toward the seep hole. He stopped under the bigger of the pecan trees, laid the reins loose on the dun's neck, then took hold of a low limb. As he swung himself up, he gave the horse a kick. It trotted on to the water trough and dunked its muzzle.

There had been a tree house in the pecan once, back when Jess was just a half-pint tad. It had only been a few planks nailed over a strong fork, with a piece of paulin for a roof. The paulin was long gone to rags and rot, and the boards were warped now, but they were still sturdy enough to bear his weight. He climbed up and seated himself with one boot dangling and the other resting on a branch of the fork. Leaning his back against the bole of the tree, he plucked a leaf and cut it carefully along a vein with his thumbnail as he waited.

Mrs. Deke contemplated awhile, then said soft and slow, "Jan, your brother's up the tree again."

January glanced over her shoulder at the tree. Sighing, she set down the bowl of corn.

"It's been a time since he's done that," she said.

Mrs. Deke considered saying something in reply. But it was too much trouble. She just kept rocking.

The chickens scurried away as January slipped down off the porch. Jess watched her stride across the yard. He'd known she'd come. She was the only one who could do anything with him when he was in one of these moods. Before she'd reached the tree, he set his eyes straight ahead.

"Jesse?" she called as she wiped her hands on her apron.

He didn't answer. He never did the first time. Not when he was really sulking.

"Jesse?"

He decided his worries this time were worth a good spell of stubborn silence. Setting his mouth firm, he waited.

"Jesse, you hear me?" There was concern in her voice, and in her dark, sad horse-eyes. When he didn't answer her this time, she tucked up her skirts and started to climb toward him. When she reached the tree house, he was just sitting there staring intently at nothing in particular.

"Jesse, didn't you hear me holler?" she said.

He nodded slightly.

January seated herself next to Jess, hanging her legs over the edge of the tree house. She looked down at the shadows of the leaves on the ground below. They made right pretty patterns, she thought. Then she noticed the very large one that didn't belong. She looked up for its source.

Pointing at the huge black bulk half-hidden in the high branches, she said, "Jesse, look there at that big old turkey buzzard."

Jess flinched at her words. He spotted the bird and glowered at it.

"That's the same damn bird. I'd swear it," he said.

"What bird?"

"That buzzard. It's been hanging around over my head all day. I'd nigh swear it was following me."

January lifted a brow at the vulture, wondering if it could be an omen of some kind. She asked, "Jesse, you in trouble?"

He nodded.

"What kind?"

"I ain't sure yet. Maybe with the law. Maybe with Hash Harker."

"Don't neither way sound too good."

"No."

"What happened?"

He sighed, then said, "Jody went and shot Whisk Shaker."

"Dead?"

"No."

"But bad, though?"

"No."

"How, then?"

"Didn't barely just nick his arm."

"That ain't no trouble, Jesse. Whisk ain't gonna be mad over nothing simple like that."

"Ain't just that," he mumbled.

With stirrings of impatience, she said, "Well, what happened?"

He shrugged, not quite sure where to begin. The beginning, maybe.

"When we got into town this morning, we went on over to Dominic's saloon and he opened up for us, and we set a few rounds and got to talking. Dom told us as how Hash Harker was expecting this Miss Lucinda Cummins of Fairwater, Virginia, that he plans to marry, in on the coach today. Dom and Jacob got to talking about it and Hash and what a high-stepping cock old Hash thinks he is, and all, and next thing I knowed, Jacob had up and bet Dom an eagle that he'd get a kiss off her before Hash did."

He stopped suddenly.

January gave a little grunt of acknowledgment to encourage him.

"We went on up the road to stop the coach and get Jacob his kiss," he told her. "Only while we was doing it, Jody up and fired off his gun and hit Whisk in the arm."

"I don't see how the law'd come into it," she said. "If Whisk ain't hurt bad, he won't complain. Not against us Wileys. Him and Pa been friends too long for that."

Jess nodded, but he didn't seem cheered. He went on, "Only there was this old bulldog of a lady with Miss Cummins, and a little drummer-looking man in one of them derby hats, and both of them was hollering at us about fetching the law and hanging us all and such things. They was noisy enough about it; I'm fearful they just might do it."

"All on account of Jacob kissing this Miss Cummins?"

"He didn't kiss her."

"What? You mean you up and stopped the coach and shot Whisk and everything and didn't even win the bet?"

"I ain't sure. After Jacob lit off without he'd done it, I kissed her myself. Only I don't know if Dom will count that fair or not."

"He ought to. You're a Wiley, ain't you? What you do for Jacob ought to count the same as if he'd done it himself."

"That's what I was figuring then," he said. "But there's times I ain't sure. Sometimes I wonder if it shouldn't be a man's place to answer for his doings himself instead of having all his kinfolk do it for him."

"Jesse Wiley! You know what Pa'd say if he heard you talk like that?"

"I know."

"Jacob and Jody is your own brothers, your own blood, and it's your bounden born duty to back them."

"I reckon," he mumbled.

She smiled smugly.

"You really expect the law'll come messing around here on account of something no bigger'n that?" she asked.

"I don't know. What if them folks what was on the coach complain to the company?"

"If you didn't take nothing, and Whisk ain't hurt, the coach-company folk'll just sweet-talk them and then forget it."

"Yeah, but there's Harker, and he's got all them friends of his he's always talking about off to the county seat and the state capital and all. If *he* goes complaining to the coach company, there won't be no sweet talk. They'll *do* something. They'll put it into the hands of the sheriff. Then he'll have to do something, and he sure ain't gonna come all the way out here to settle it himself, so he's bound to send for a Ranger. And they just ain't very easygoing at all. One of them comes around, Pa'll get mad, and there'll be hell to pay."

Catching his breath, Jess lapsed into a sullen silence.

January pursed her lips as she considered the situation. Admittedly, Hash Harker was a sawed-off dandy, but he was a man of considerable influence in this end of the county. Maybe even in the whole of Texas, for all she knew. She did know that he had strings tied to the capital, and he could pull them if he took a notion. There was no telling what he might do if he got riled. And there was no telling what her brothers might do if they got spooked.

She asked, "Where are they?"

"Who?" Jess grunted.

"Jacob and Jody."

"Last I seen of them, they was taking off toward town."

"Why'd they do that?"

"To get drunk, I reckon. They had a notion

they'd killed Whisk, and didn't neither one of them stay around long enough to find out different."

"Oh, Jesse!" She sounded real disappointed in him.

He looked at her from the corner of his eye. "What?"

"You mean to tell me you left those two poor boys wandering around thinking they'd done something like that?"

"Likely they've found out different by now."

"What if they haven't? They'll be worried purely sick."

"Let 'em worry."

"Jesse Wiley! They're your *brothers!*"

Sighing, Jess glanced up. The buzzard was still there in the treetop. It hadn't stirred. He snapped a bit of twig from a branch. Taking careful aim, he flung it at the bird.

With an indignant squawk, the vulture spread its huge black wings. It abandoned its perch in the tree and flapped noisily toward the sun.

The creaking of the rocker on the porch stopped. A faint frown added to the creases in Mrs. Deke's forehead. She thought she'd heard the beating of wings. Big wings, right close by.

Mrs. Deke knew an omen when she met one. She'd been born almost with a caul. She could hear the ticking of ghostly watches within walls, and could tell who the screech owls cried after. She saw shadows and felt cold winds where nobody else could. Folks all agreed she had a

38

special *feeling* for unnatural things.

She had a *feeling* now.

Death.

And Mr. Wiley.

She ran her tongue over her lips as she pondered the omen. After a moment, she took a sip of laudanum. Resettling the bottle in her lap, she leaned back and began to rock slowly. Thoughtfully.

The creak of the old chair was familiar and reassuring. Her memories were warm and comforting. She knew with a certainty that Mr. Wiley would never leave her, no matter what happened. Alive or dead, he'd be back soon.

CHAPTER 4

Jess had taken a fresh mount. The spotty-rumped blue roan. He was riding easy, his thoughts drifting, when he noticed the vulture. It was high overhead, and moving in much the same direction as he was. He felt almost as if the damned thing were following him on purpose.

When he reached the wagon road, he turned toward Hardly. He had a notion he'd like to turn the other way and just keep going. He didn't figure he'd do it, though. All the times he'd thought about packing out, he'd never done anything about it. He supposed he never would. He'd go on into Hardly and find his brothers and see what kind of trouble might be shaping up. He didn't expect he'd have any difficulty locating Jacob and Jody. Likely they'd head straight for the saloon.

Dominic Johanssen's Grand Palace of the Golden Dragon (formerly the Grand American Palace Saloon) was about the fanciest place in all of Hardly. It looked like a first-class steamboat. The galleries on the front were trimmed with twiddly gingerbread woodwork, and the inside, what could be seen of it in the dim lamplight Dominic provided, was a pleasure to the eye.

The walls were paneled in polished wood, the bar and backbar decorated with hand-carved mahogany do-diddles. The backbar mirror was as tall as a man, twice that wide, and cracked in only a couple of places. The lamps hanging from the ceiling were brass with glass danglies. Red plush drapes with tassels decorated all the windows, even the tiny ones in the little rooms upstairs.

Admittedly, the Grand Palace of the Golden Dragon wasn't exactly palatial in every way. The saloon itself was about the size and shape of a small boxcar. The little rooms upstairs were barely large enough for a cot to be squeezed into each of them. But the whole place did break down and pack flat on wagons for shipping, a fact Dominic was right proud of.

The structure had begun its days when Granville Dodge was building the Union Pacific. As the railroad moved from point to point, so did the saloon. When the transcontinental railway was completed, the saloon had moved on to the end-of-track on Cy Holliday's Atchison & Topeka line. There, in a sudden-death hand of high-low-jack, it had become the property of Dominic Johanssen.

One day Dominic Johanssen heard Big Jim Boohm, the Builder, speechifying about how the best way to get ahead in the getting-rich business was to be on just the right spot before a railhead arrived. Big Jim recommended Hardly as the spot to be on. Dominic, a man of mighty dreams

41

and ambitions, had taken Big Jim's advice to heart. He'd taken his saloon to Hardly.

Being a man of deep faith and perseverance as well as dreams and ambitions, Dominic was still on the spot, patiently waiting. He was waiting behind the bar in the Grand Palace of the Golden Dragon, swabbing at dirty glasses with a dirty rag when Jess Wiley came in through the back door.

Jess glanced around. Neither of his brothers was in evidence. The only other people in the saloon were the two old men seated by the front window. They were too engrossed in their own conversation to notice anything much, even Jess's arrival.

Dominic noticed. He called to Jess, " 'Morning. I'm sure glad you come back. I got to talk to you, Jesse. I got a problem."

"Later. You seen Jacob or Jody around?"

"Not since the three of you took off from here this morning to meet the coach. Did Jacob kiss Hash Harker's ladyfriend like he set out to do?"

"Kinda."

"What you mean, *kinda?* Either you kiss a gal or you don't."

"That's just it," Jess told him. "It was *me* as kissed her. That counts the same as if Jacob done it, don't it?"

"You ain't Jacob."

"I'm a Wiley, though, same as him. I done it in his name."

"But — oh, hell, I don't know," Dominic said. He sighed and twisted at an end of his magnificent yellow moustache. "Jesse, I just ain't up to worrying over it right now. I got another problem. I got to talk to you."

"Later," Jess said again. He turned toward the staircase to the upper floor.

Doors painted with red lead stood in solemn ranks along the narrow upstairs hallway. He rapped gently at the second one on his left. There was no response. He hit it again, harder.

"Unh?" a sleepy female voice called from within.

"Nance?" he said.

"Unh?"

"It's me."

"Unh."

Floorboards creaked. The door opened. A face appeared. Under its coating of Professor Bonneville's Magnolia Oil Complexion Lotion, the face was very young. The hair wrapped in bright red rag curlers was as naturally blond as a tow-headed child's.

She clutched her calico wrapper closed at the throat and frowned blurrily at Jess. "You're early, ain't you?"

"Uh-huh. No. Not exactly. I mean, I come by to tell you I likely won't be able to get by today," he told her.

"Oh," she said, and the word slid off into a yawn.

"Something's come up," Jess continued.

"Likely I won't get to see you again before to-morrow."

"You still gonna take me to the partying to-morrow?"

"Uh-huh."

"All right. But I got to finish my sleep now," she said, stepping back. She closed the door.

As Jess headed downstairs, he was thinking she sounded like she didn't really care. And then he was wondering if *he* really cared.

He walked over to the bar and leaned on it.

Dominic set down the glass he'd been polishing. Mournfully, he said, "Jesse, I got a problem."

"You ain't the only one," Jess mumbled.

"It's that sister of yours."

"Junie? What's the matter with her?"

"She . . . she . . ." Dominic darted a quick glance around, as if he were fearful of eavesdroppers. But the only other people in the room were the two old men by the window. One was a vinegarroon named Ezekiel W. Trot. The other was the Reverend P. Jonathan Seven. Both were rapt in their own discussion. Neither paid any attention to the men at the bar.

Whispering conspiratorially, Dominic said, "She's in the family way."

Jess's lips spread back over his large yellow teeth in a delighted grin. He clapped a hand on Dominic's shoulder. "Congratulations!"

Dominic shook his head sadly.

"What's wrong?" Jess asked. "Ain't it yours?"

"She claims it ain't. But damn if I can see how she's got any sure idea whose it is. I swear it's as likely mine as anybody's."

"Likely," Jess said sympathetically.

"That don't matter none, though," Dominic told him. "I don't care whose it is, long as it's a nice fat little young'un what'll call me Pa when it starts in talking."

"Then what's troubling you so?"

"It's Junie, that's what. She *still* won't marry me."

"Look here, Dom, what difference does it make? It ain't like she won't haul your water and chop the cooking wood, is it?"

"Oh, she's a fine woman, all right. Ain't a wife in the world does any better by her man than Junie does for me. Weren't for that, I'd likely be out hunting me some other gal. One that would marry me. But I'm used to Junie now, and she's just fine around the house. Only it ain't right somehow. It'd sure pride me if I could rightly call her Missus Johanssen. Ever since I was just a speck of a tadpole, that's what I wanted me. A fancy preacher-wedding with a shivaree afterwards, and a little woman to share my name." Dominic paused to catch his breath, then added, "That's something right special, Jesse."

"I reckon," Jess muttered. He sure couldn't see it himself, though. "Look, Dom, I got to find my brothers. You think maybe Junie's seen them?"

"I don't know."

"Is she likely at home now?"

"I don't know. She was in here awhile ago. Come by for a quick breakfast drink with me. That's when she told me about the baby. I asked her to marry me. Jesse, I've asked her and asked her and asked her, every which way I been able to think of, and it's got to where I've got to where I'm starting to repeat myself, and she just sets there and yawns. I ain't getting no younger, Jesse. I want me a wife."

"Uh-huh. I'll go see if she's home." Jess touched his hat brim and started to turn away.

"Speak to her, will you, Jesse?" Dominic said. "Tell her how it is with me. Explain to her. Ask her won't she please marry me. You're her brother, and older'n she is. Maybe you can talk her into it."

"Pomegranate!" Ezekiel W. Trot hollered from his corner by the window.

The Reverend P. Jonathan Seven shook his head in denial and said, "Apple!"

"If you can talk her into it, I'll name the baby after you. If it's a boy," Dominic called at Jess's back.

Jess nudged the door open. As he stepped outside, he could hear Dominic still shouting at him.

"Even if it's a girl! If it's a girl, we'll call it Jessica."

He strode on into the yard and collected his horse. It rolled a white-rimmed eye at him as he swung on board. He rode the few paces from the

46

back of the saloon to the little clapboard cottage on the rise.

"Hallo! Junie!" he hollered as he ambled the roan up to the house. Halting, he stepped from the saddle onto the back porch and looped the reins around a corner post. The back door was standing open. He started for it.

"Jesse?" Junie called as she came through the door.

As a child, Junie Wiley'd had the good fortune of an illness that stunted her growth and caused several of her brand-new adult jaw teeth to fall out. Now, she stood barely head high to Jess's shoulder. Her bones were light and delicate instead of long and knobby as was usual with the Wileys. Nourishment that might have gone into stretching her frame had, instead, fleshed it out. And, having space to spread, her large square teeth had grown straight instead of thrusting aggressively forward. Her body was small and well-rounded. Her smile was even and well-shaped. She was the pride of the Wiley bunch, far and away the handsomest of them all.

She held out her hands and beamed at her brother. "Oh, Jesse, I'm so glad you happened by! I've got the greatest news!"

"About the baby?" he said, grinning. He took her hands in his.

"How did you know? Did Ma vision it?"

"No. Dom just told me."

"That Dominic! I swear, he ain't got no business telling everybody *my* surprise."

"He figures it's his business."

She tugged her hands. He let them slide out of his grip. She shaped them into small fists and held them up as if she threatened him. But her wispy anger was aimed at Dominic.

"It ain't his business, and I told him so. It ain't like it was *his* baby."

"How you know it ain't his?"

"I know. I can tell. I got a feeling."

"You're just guessing," he teased.

She shook her head solemnly. "There's things a mother just sort of *knows* somehow. She feels it inside. Jesse, you want to come in and set awhile? I'll make us some tea."

"Can't stay long," he said as he pulled off his hat and followed her into the house.

In the parlor, he settled himself into the over-stuffed cushion chair and set his boots up on the hassock. Junie went to the big stained-oak sideboard and lit the tea lamp. She filled the kettle and set it on the frame of the lamp to heat. While she was waiting for the water to boil, she set out the teacups in their tiny saucers and carefully prepared the pot. The tea service was white with blue-limned pictures of pagodas and willow trees and tiny figures hurrying across humpbacked bridges in exotic gardens. Dominic cherished them above almost all of his other possessions.

Dominic had a passion for all things Oriental. One of his most deeply rooted ambitions was to someday visit China, a land he envisioned as filled with perky-eaved pagodas like those on the tea set, and minaret-topped mosques such as he'd seen in a steel engraving titled *Oriental Dream.* To Dominic the Orient was the Orient.

Holding the precious teapot in both hands, Junie turned to face her brother.

"Jesse," she said, "I've got a problem."

He looked up at her. "About the baby?"

"About Dominic. He keeps on asking me to marry him."

"I know. Why don't you do it?"

"I don't want to."

"He asked me to talk to you about it," Jess told her. "Said if I'd talk you into it, he'd name the baby after me."

She smiled a small secret smile as she shook her head. "Can't. I already decided what I'm gonna name him."

"You know for sure it's gonna be a *him?*"

"I got a feeling."

"Something a mother just sort of knows?"

"Uh-huh."

"What you figure on calling him?"

"Hash."

He frowned in surprise. "Like in Hash Harker?"

Her smile got all twisty at the corners, and she nodded slightly. Jess could have sworn she was blushing. He'd never seen her do that before. He cocked his head and gazed in question at her.

"I think the water's about ready," she said, though the kettle hadn't made a sound. She turned her back to him. For a few moments she puttered with things that didn't need doing.

Suddenly she said, "It ain't that I don't like Dominic, but it just . . . he . . . Jesse, what I want in a man is that he *needs* me."

Jess wasn't sure whether he'd actually made a promise to speak in Dominic's behalf, but he reckoned he ought to. "Dom needs you, sis. Who'd tend his house and take care of him if you wasn't here?"

"Somebody. Anybody. It ain't *me* Dom cares about. It's just the notion of being married. Any girl would do him, as long as she'd be Mrs. Johanssen. All he really wants is to have him a preacher-spoke wife. If I ever let myself be bespoke, it'll be for more than that."

"You really fancy Hash Harker?" he asked her.

She hesitated, then gave her head a quick little bob.

"You know he's already got this Miss Lucinda Cummins of Fairwater, Virginia, promised to him?"

She nodded again.

He sighed.

The kettle began to growl.

As Junie got the tea started brewing, she asked, "Ma and Jan coming in to the partying tomorrow?"

"Uh-huh."

"Don't tell them about the baby, Jesse. Let me surprise them."

"Sure."

Remembering his own problem, he asked,

"You seen Jacob or Jody this afternoon?"

"No."

She remembered something then herself. Looking askance at him, she said, "Jesse, I heard some talk that the three of you stopped Whisk Shaker's coach and shot at him."

"Uh-huh."

"What'd you do that for? Whisk ain't never got worthwhile money on his coach."

"I know. Wasn't for the money."

"What for, then?"

"Just horsing around," he told her.

"Oh." She supposed that was as good a reason as any. "Like a muffin with your tea?"

"Uh-huh."

She fetched a napkin-covered basket and set it within easy reach on the taboret beside his chair. He lifted the napkin and helped himself to a muffin.

Junie checked the tea. It looked ready. She poured two cups almost half full, then topped them off with brandy.

Jess accepted the one she held out to him. He sipped and smiled. The tea was as good as usual. Nobody else could brew a pot of tea the way Junie could, he thought as he drained the cup. He set it on the taboret and wiped at the muffin crumbs on his chin, then got to his feet.

"Going so soon?" June asked him.

"Got to."

"Can't you stay for another cup?"

"Like to. But there's things I got to tend."

"Can't they wait awhile?"

" 'Fraid not." He took another muffin and crammed it into his vest pocket for later.

"Tell Ma I'm looking forward to seeing her," Junie said. "But remember, don't tell her no more than that."

"Yes'm." He nodded, touched his hat brim to her, and left.

She poured herself another cup of tea.

CHAPTER 5

As Jess stepped out onto the porch, he spotted the vulture again. It was perched on the roof of the carriage house, looking for all the world as if it were waiting there for him.

He felt certain now that it was some kind of omen. Likely the worst kind. He reached for his gun.

The buzzard spread its wings and jerked itself into the sky.

Jess stood watching as it disappeared behind the carriage house. He told himself that he'd get it the next time. If that damned buzzard showed up, he'd get it for sure.

He still had his hand on the gun and his thoughts on the buzzard when he noticed the way the mare in the corral was acting. She shuffled restlessly, sniffing and snuffling at the carriage-house door, carrying on like she scented a strange horse.

He wondered if his brothers could be hiding in the stable. Or maybe it was something else, like a horse thief. That mare was a fine animal. One he would have considered himself if it hadn't been owned so close to the family.

The big wagon doors at the front of the carriage house were ajar. He walked softly over and paused just outside. His fingers were still on the butt of the revolver. Drawing it, he rested his thumb against the hammer, leaned forward, and looked into the gloom of the shed.

There was a horse inside, half-hidden behind Dominic's shay. He recognized the black and white rump of the little pinto mare he'd cut out of a mustang herd when it was a yearling.

Glancing around, he called, "July?"

There was a faint noise. From within the shay, he thought. Eyes peered at him from the darkness under the raised top of the rig. Two pairs of them.

"July," he repeated, his voice less a question, more a demand this time. He walked on into the shed, the revolver still muzzle-up in his hand. "Come down out of there."

"Won't!"

It was his kid sister, all right, sounding as stubborn as usual.

"Come down," he said.

"Else what?"

He thumbed the gun hammer back to half-cock. The click of it was loud in the dark hollows of the shed. It echoed and faded into silence. July's stubborn silence.

He brought the hammer back to full cock.

"You won't," July said.

Aiming carefully, well clear of the eyes in the shadows, he pulled the trigger.

The thunder of the shot rattled around inside

the shed. Stinging powder smoke puffed into his face. The high-sprung shay trembled on its gaunt wheels.

"Allah!" a boy's voice squeaked.

July answered it with a harsh whisper. "Don't let him spook you, Hassan. Pa'd give him all hell in a fry pan if he was to shoot us."

"*You*, maybe," the boy said. "But your pa don't care camel dung if he shoots *me*."

July sighed with audible scorn.

From the porch Junie hollered, "Jesse, that you shooting?"

"Yeah," he shouted back.

"Anything wrong?"

"No."

"All right." Junie's voice faded as she headed back into the house for another cup of tea.

Jess looked at the eyes in the shay. "What you two doing in there anyway?"

"Messing around," July said.

Hassan spoke up. "We was waiting for you."

"You leave a trail a blind jackass with its nose cut off could follow in the dark of night during a sandstorm with its head inside a gunny sack," July told her brother.

"What you been following me for?" he asked.

"Fun. You going anywhere from here, Jesse?"

"You plan to track me there, too?"

"Sure."

"Rightly you ought to be home helping January."

"You know, Hassan, I got a problem," July

55

said, her voice heavy with mock weariness. Her words were aimed at Jess.

"What?" Hassan asked her.

"I'm a *girl,* that's what."

Jess said, "How's that a problem?"

She turned directly to him. "You'd let me go with you places if I wasn't a girl. All the time you take Jody everywhere —"

"He's older'n you," Jess interrupted.

"I know. But he ain't near as smart as me. I'd be a lot more help to you, but you never take me along nowhere. Even when you go out stopping coaches, you take that dumb old Jody and let him shoot people and cause a ruckus, but you wouldn't even take me along to the crick to fetch water."

"How'd you know about that business with the coach?" Jess asked.

"I got my ways," she said wisely.

"You been visioning?"

In reply, she gave a noncommittal snort. He reckoned that might mean she couldn't honestly say *yes.* On the other hand, she just naturally lied a lot, so maybe it didn't exactly mean *no* either.

"You really been visioning?" Hassan asked her.

She didn't answer him.

Jess said, "Maybe I would take you someplace sometime if you wasn't always stealing my cartridges."

"Coach robbing?" she asked eagerly.

He imitated her noncommittal snort.

She suggested, "Maybe down to Mexico to pick up a herd? I sure would like to see that cantina Jacob's always talking about."

He snorted again.

"Where, Jesse? Please, where you gonna take me? When? Soon? Huh?"

Hesitantly, Hassan said, "Maybe I could go too?"

"I said *maybe*," Jess answered. "*If* you wasn't always emptying my gun while my back was turned."

July drew a deep breath while she thought up a reply. She decided that the best defense was an attack. On somebody.

"Maybe if you didn't go giving Jody more bullets after I took his, he wouldn't go around shooting people and getting everybody in trouble. What you gonna do if a Ranger comes around, Jesse? You know what Pa's gonna say."

"That's none of your business."

"Is, too. I'm a Wiley, even if I am a girl. We're all together in everything, ain't we?"

Jess couldn't rightly deny that. Instead, he said, "What you always got to go stealing cartridges for anyway?"

"I ain't got no money to buy them, and there won't nobody never give me none."

"You're such a rotten shot there won't nobody trust you with a loaded gun," he said.

"How am I ever gonna get any better, 'less I practice a lot?" she protested.

She had a point there, he owned to himself.

He wouldn't tell her that, though. Grabbing at a passing idea, he said, "How'd you like a chance to get some practice?"

"Sure!"

"Got your gun with you?"

She nodded warily. She'd been forbidden to carry a gun.

"I got a little job for you," Jess said. He thumbed back the gate on his revolver. There were four loads in it. He began prying them out. "There's a big ornery old turkey buzzard been following me around all day. You put a few of these into it and I'll buy you six more rounds all your own."

Hassan said, "I think it's bad luck to kill a buzzard."

"No, it ain't!" July hollered. She came scrambling down from the shay and grabbed the cartridges out of Jess's hand. "I'll fetch back that old bird on a platter for you!"

July was obviously a Wiley. She had the Wiley look of too many teeth, lots of long knobby bones, and not much in the line of flesh. The dress she wore was a hand-me-down from Mrs. Deke to January to Junie to her. It was the dull gray of faded dyes and ground-in grime, and it hung on her like an empty feed sack, barely suggesting that she'd begun to turn from child into woman.

Hassan slipped from the darkness of the shay and stepped to her side. He was dark of hair and eye, with a gentle mouth and a strong jaw. He had a shyness about him, but July figured he'd grow out of that. She expected that in time, with the right guidance from someone like her, he'd make up into a fine man.

Hassan's mother, Dawn Woman, was Mojave. His father, who called himself simply Ali Ibn, was Arabian and something of a hakim. Ali Ibn was the town's pharmacist and, on occasion, its physician. Hassan had learned a lot from them both.

He spoke up. "I know ways of baiting birds. I can get things from my Pa's shop to put into a bait as will strike that old buzzard dead."

"I don't care how you do it," Jess said. He didn't really think they'd manage to kill the bird. Not with July's aim. But maybe they'd succeed in scaring it off. "You just stop it from following me everywhere."

July had produced a forty-five-caliber artillery-model Colt revolver from somewhere within her clothing. As she shoved the rounds into the cylinder, she mumbled, "You know, Jesse, as brothers go, I reckon you ain't always the worst in the world."

He grinned at her.

"Likely there's a lot better somewhere, though," she added. "But at least you ain't as bad as Jody or Jacob."

Jess turned his back on her with a grunt.

She followed him through the door of the shed and watched him collect his roan. As he rose to the saddle, she shouted at him, "You still looking for Jacob and Jody?"

"Yeah."

"They're hid out over to Coyote Gulch, in that secret place you-all used to hide in when you was kids."

"You seen them there?"

She shook her head.

"She knows, though," Hassan said.

Jess decided the boy was probably right. July seemed to be developing a way for *feeling* things, same as her Ma had. A mite proud of his little sister, he touched his hat brim to her.

"Obliged."

"I wouldn't of told you, only you give me them bullets," she hollered.

He gigged the roan and headed it for Main Street. Before he went after his brothers, he figured he'd better stock up on some more ammunition.

CHAPTER 6

The town of Hardly hadn't turned out quite the way Big Jim Boohm envisioned it. Gaps among the buildings on Main Street showed where he had platted a number of cross streets, but now they served only as access to backyards and as grazing places for several goats. The lone existing cross street — Sixth Street, according to official documents — survived because the wagon route ran along it.

Jess Wiley drew rein in front of the massive building at the corner of Sixth and Main. A creaking, weather-worn sight proclaimed the impressive structure to house "Dudley's Gen. Mdse." He tied the roan to the sagging hitch rein in front of the store, ambled up to the open door, and discovered that there were customers ahead of him.

The huge main room of the store was lit by one lone Rochester lamp hung from the ceiling. When there were customers, which wasn't often, the proprietor, McDonald Dudley, fired up a hand lantern and carried it to whatever counter was of immediate interest. Two women bent their heads together as they examined and discussed spools of braid by lantern light at the notions counter.

McDonald Dudley was leaning his elbows on the counter and nodding like a half-dozing horse while he awaited their decision. The sight of another customer in the doorway jolted him. Business was seldom so brisk.

The women, holding the spools of braid close to the lantern to compare them, paid no attention to Jess. He was glad of that. He recognized them both.

He gestured for Dudley to stay with them, and hurried on across the store to lose himself in the darkness of the hardware department.

Mrs. Delphinia Quick (widowed) decided on plum-colored braid and a pair of matching frogs. Miss Lucinda Cummins then pointed to a bolt of flannel that looked gray in the shadows. She asked if she might see it in the light.

Dudley lifted down the yard goods and stood with the bolt cradled in his arms while the ladies preceded him through the doorway. Out in the sunlight, he unrolled an arm's length of the fabric. It proved to be a dusty green.

Mrs. Delphinia Quick bent close over it, squinting at the weave.

Miss Lucinda Cummins glanced back at the dark maw of the store and said, "Oh, I've left my reticule on the counter."

Clutching her skirts, she scurried back inside.

Oblivious of her departure, Mrs. Delphinia said, "You *must* be more careful, child. This isn't Fairwater, Virginia, you know. There isn't any telling what cut-purses and horsepads may be lurking in the shadows awaiting the opportunity to snatch the very rings off your fingers."

But at that moment, Miss Lucinda wasn't concerned with her finger rings. Or her reticule, for that matter. She was holding up the hand lantern Dudley had left on the counter, and was scanning the dark at the back of the store.

In a soft squeak she called, "Mr. Wiley?"

Hopeful that the ladies would leave without ever noticing him, Jess had squeezed himself between a display rack of rifles and the stuffed remains of a bedraggled bull bison with mournful glass eyes and a price tag so old and faded that the figures on it had disappeared completely. At the sound of his name from Miss Lucinda's lips, he flinched. His elbow brushed the bison. It shuddered, threatening to disintegrate. He steadied it with his hand as he leaned forward to peer past its rump at the girl in the puddle of lantern light.

"I saw you come in," Miss Lucinda announced to the darkness. "I know you're in here somewhere."

"Yes'm," Jess mumbled. She seemed to have him cornered. Cautiously he stepped around the end of the bison with his hat in one hand and his revolver in the other. The hat covered the gun. He didn't want to scare Miss Lucinda unless she scared him first.

She lifted the lantern higher. Its glow reached toward him. Taking two quick steps forward,

63

she captured him in the edge of its light.

"Mr. Wiley, I've got to speak to you," she said. "I've got a problem."

He frowned at her in surprise.

With a bit of a stammer she began, "I — I am rather well-read."

He'd always suspicioned that reading could cause problems, but he'd never investigated the matter. He had no idea what she might want him to do about it.

"I've read a good deal concerning this part of the country, and persons like yourself. I know it isn't necessarily costume or appearance that denotes a gentleman, or even station and breeding." The flow of carefully rehearsed words emboldened her. She took another step toward him. "The truly gentlemanly soul may on occasion occur in even the most base-born."

With a flash of inspiration, she interrupted herself to ad-lib, "You can't always tell a book by its cover."

He nodded slightly, wondering what she was talking about.

She looked up into his eyes. "I know, sir, that despite your appearance, you are truly a gentle-man."

He licked his lips and blinked at her.

"I could tell instantly from the way you . . . you — er — you *looked* at me, there by the stage-coach." She was losing track of her speech. Suddenly she heard herself blurt out, "I've almost

made a terrible mistake! I *will* make one if someone doesn't help me. You must help me, Mr.
Wiley!"

"Huh?"

"It's Mr. Harker. He — I — oh, he's very nice,
and I'm sure he and I — but — I can't *marry*
him. Not now that I've — I've . . ."

She groped for the phrase. It had been in that
book about Rosalind and Theodore. She was
certain it was on the page opposite the lovely
steel engraving of the rose-entwined bower behind the north wing of the stately old manor
house. The picture was vivid in her mind, the
lattices and rosebuds and the quaint marble of
Young Eros with Figleaf on his fluted pedestal under the lilacs. But the words . . .

At last they came to her. "Now that I've sipped
the sweet nectar fresh-sprung from the heart's
own fount of true love!"

"Huh?" Jess said. His palms felt sweaty. He
wanted to wipe them, but his hands were occupied with his hat and revolver.

Miss Lucinda exclaimed, "You must take me
away from all this!"

The gun slid out of Jess's grip. It clattered on
the floor.

Startled, Miss Lucinda dropped the lantern.
She flung herself against Jess, her arms locking
tight around his neck.

For an instant she was hanging onto him as if
he were a floating log in a flooded stream. Then
her hold became something softer. More yield-

ing. She nestled warmly against him.

"Cindy!"

The shocked cry kicked Miss Lucinda like a mule. Jess felt her wince and go tense. He looked over her shoulder.

The lantern had landed on its base. It stood on the floor, still burning, casting its light toward the doorway. Its glow lit the glistening whites of the eyes of Mrs. Delphinia Quick (widowed). She took a breath and reared back her shoulders, filling the doorway.

"You!" she said, glowering at Jess. "Unhand that child!"

Miss Lucinda's grip on Jess collapsed. She staggered back from him, gaunt and white as if he'd struck her. Slowly, she turned to face her chaperon.

Jess discovered that he'd dropped his hat as well as his gun. Stooping, he recovered them both. He holstered the gun, set the hat on his head, and touched the brim of it politely to the woman in the doorway.

From somewhere behind Mrs. Delphinia's looming bulk, McDonald Dudley called, " 'Evening, Jess. Is there something I can do for you?"

" 'Evening, Dud," Jess answered. "I've took a box of forty-five cartridges off the shelf. You can put them on my bill."

"Glad to," Dudley said.

"Horsepad! Poltroon! Despoiler!" Mrs. Delphinia shrieked dutifully. She had gotten up a good head of steam. Her voice filled the room

66

and spilled over into the street. "Mr. Harker shall hear of this!"

Jess glanced around. The woman had the front door pretty well blocked. He looked toward Dudley's living quarters. There was a back way out through there. He went for it.

He slammed the door behind him and hurried around the building to collect his horse. When he got there, Mrs. Delphinia was still filling the entrance, still shouting. Her body shook with every word. From the rear, she was an impressive sight. Several people had come to look.

Jess returned nods of greeting and reached for the roan's reins. That was when he spotted Hash Harker. And Harker caught sight of him.

Harker had been ambling toward the store, where he had arranged to meet his fiancée and her chaperon to take them to tea. He'd been preoccupied with the problems his mail-order bride and her huge companion posed. The old woman had raised hell in a hogshead about what had happened with the coach outside of town. He supposed he was honor-bound to do something about those Wiley boys, and he knew what his course of action should be. He was rehearsing a suitable speech as prologue to it when he saw one of them right there on the corner ahead of him.

"Wiley!" he hollered, waving and breaking into a trot. "Jesse Wiley! Hold on a minute!"

Jogging up, he halted in front of Jess. He was a good ten years older, and maybe four inches shorter. Looking up into Jess's face, he shifted his weight from one foot to the other, and tugged at the shaggy tuft of a sandy tan sideburn. He'd rehearsed his speech, but now it didn't want to come.

"Jess," he blurted. "I've got a problem."

If Jess had been asked to name forty-seven things Hash Harker might say to him, he would never have included that. It surprised him into a bewildered grunt.

Harker took the grunt for an encouraging reply. He continued, "You are aware, of course, that I am a gentleman come from a long line of fine old Southern famblies?"

Jess nodded. He'd heard as much, and he'd never had cause to doubt it.

Hash spoke with a soft Southern drawl. He owned a fine house over near the springs, and the fanciest trotting horses in the county, and a fancy collection of firearms, and kept servants to tend it all. He dressed the part, too, what with nankeen breeches and mother-of-pearl studs and yellow kid gloves. He made frequent trips into the state capital, and it was said he dined with senators and sometimes even the governor. Whatever his origins, he was the ultimate in aristocracy in Hardly, and certainly the town dandy.

Hash looked into Jess's face, then glanced around. Mrs. Delphinia was still in the doorway of the Gen. Mdse., but she'd done a full turn. Now she was watching him. So was Miss

Lucinda. So were all the other folk who'd gathered to see what was happening.

Clearing his throat, Hash took hold of his resolve and went on. "A gentleman like me's got obligations, Jesse. I mean, there's matters he's got to respect, no matter what. You know that?"

Jess nodded.

"I believe you are aware that I'm engaged to a lady name of Miss Lucinda Cummins of Fairwater, Virginia?"

"Uh-huh."

"In fact, I believe you've met Miss Cummins?"

"Kinda."

"As I understand it, you and your brothers stopped the coach today by force, and shot the driver grievously, and you yourself — ah — er — committed a breach of gentlemanly conduct toward Miss Cummins."

"I reckon you might could say that," Jess mumbled.

"I want you to understand this ain't anything personal, Jesse. It's my bounden duty as a gentleman. You've — uh — insulted my fiancy, and I've got to do something about it. I mean, a man's got to do things in the proper way, no matter what. You know what I mean?"

Jess didn't, but he nodded anyway.

"I'm glad you understand and agree," Hash said, drawing off one soft yellow glove.

He slapped Jess across the face with it.

Jess hit him with a fist.

Mouth agape, Hash staggered back. He tripped and fell sprawling.

Looking down at him, Jess had a notion maybe hitting him that way hadn't been quite the proper thing. But it had come natural, without he'd planned it. He started to offer Hash a hand up. But then, suddenly, Mrs. Delphinia was confronting him.

"Of all the vile, low, uncivilized, ungentlemanly, barbarian behavior!" she puffed at him. "I never!"

Harker clambered to his feet unassisted. He picked up the glove he'd dropped and used it to brush at the dust on his breeches. When he faced Jess again, it was with an expression of hurt dignity rather than anger.

"My second will call on you this evening," he said staunchly. Wheeling, he marched toward the store. Mrs. Delphinia followed him like an escort of heavy dragoons.

Pushing through the assembled spectators, Matt Matthews faced Jess. Awed, he said, "Jesse, you know what?"

"What?"

"Hash Harker's just up and challenged you to a duel!"

"Yeah."

Sudden mutterings rustled through the crowd. Pike Peckett waved a hand full of coin and shouted, "I got three dollars in silver what says Hash'll win!"

"I got twenty in gold says he won't," Jess hollered back.

CHAPTER 7

As Jess headed the blue roan up Sixth Street, he scanned the sky. There was a bird of some kind up there, but it was too high for him to tell whether or not it was the vulture. He had a dark feeling it was, though. That bird seemed to be dogging him.

He stayed with Sixth Street as it dwindled to a pair of wagon ruts, followed the ruts a good ways, then turned off toward the hole in the ground called Coyote Gulch. Someone was there, all right. The smoke of a campfire pointed into the hole like a tattletale finger.

The broad *llano* was crisscrossed with washes and gullies of one kind and another. Jess stayed to the high ground. He left the roan hobbled a short ways from the gulch and footed it over to the brink. Standing there, he looked down. True to July's prediction, his brothers were in the bottom of the hole. So were July and Hassan. They all huddled around a small fire with a rabbit spitted over it.

July was the one who finally noticed Jess standing there silhouetted against the sky. As she saw him, she called his name.

"Uh-huh," he answered.

71

"Jesse!" Jacob spurted with relief. "I'm sure glad to see you! What become of you? Do you know if Pa's back yet? What you reckon we ought to do now?"

"Poor old Whisk," Jody moaned. "I sure never meant to kill him."

Jacob added, "You got a bottle with you, Jesse?"

Jess shook his head. The scent of scorching rabbit stirred his juices. He felt into his pocket for the muffin he'd brought from Junie's. His fingers came up full of crumbs and lint.

"Ain't you coming down?" July called to him.

He licked his fingers, then slipped over the brink and skidded boots first down the sandy sandstone to the bottom of the gulch.

"Did you bring a bottle?" Jacob asked him again as he collected himself.

He shook his head.

"Poor old Whisk," Jody repeated.

Jacob said, "I reckon we ought to go to the burying. Don't you?"

Jess brushed at his breeches, then hunkered at July's side and darted her a slanting glance. He said, "Didn't you tell them about Whisk?"

"What about Whisk?" Jody asked.

July shook her head.

"Why not?" Jess said.

She shrugged. Her face was blank, but Jess could sense the grin she was hiding. She'd been having a lot of fun watching her brothers seethe in their own imaginings.

72

"What about Whisk?" Jody asked.

July met Jess's gaze, her eyes as wide and direct as if nary an unkind thought ever lingered behind them. But she knew he was making a good guess at her thoughts.

Her voice was as childishly innocent as her eyes. "Jesse, I couldn't find speck nor spot of that old buzzard. I got me a rabbit, though."

Hassan pointed to the carcass over the fire as proudly as if he'd been the one who bagged it.

Jess said, "How many shots it take?"

July held up two fingers. Hassan lifted a brow at her. She darted him a dark scowl. He shrank back, losing himself in her shadow.

"*What* about Whisk?" Jody demanded.

"Whisk ain't dead," Jess told him. "He ain't even decent hurt. You only just barely nicked his arm."

"Huh?" Jacob grunted.

Jess nodded. "You'd of knowed then and there if you hadn't let out so quick."

"My horse up and run away," Jacob said, as if that explained and justified everything.

Jody stared at Jess as he slowly absorbed the news. Thinly he said, "Then everything's all right now?"

Excepting for the trouble with Hash Harker, Jess thought. But there was no point in rushing things, piling more troubles on his brothers now while they were so relieved about Whisk. He could tell them about it later.

He nodded.

"The rabbit's nigh ready to eat," July said.

Jacob grinned widely. "And I'm ready to eat it!"

"Me, too!" Jody put in as he reached for the charred carcass.

Jess watched them scrabble happily for pieces of the meat. They were like kids at a partying, all full of joy for the moment. Not a one of them had a thought of trouble now.

He couldn't share their mood. He didn't feel like trying. Despite the fire, he could feel the chill that came with encroaching twilight. He felt oddly alone here with his brothers and sister.

Quietly avoiding their attention, he got to his feet and headed for his horse.

By the time Jess reached the house, the thin purple shadows of evening were disappearing into darkness.

Lamplight spilling from the parlor window gave shape to the buggy parked by the front porch, and the gray geld dozing between the shafts. He recognized the rig. Drawing rein, he shifted in the saddle and gazed speculatively at it. If Hash Harker's buggy was outside, chances were that trouble was waiting inside.

He didn't stir at the sound of a horse approaching from behind. The hooffalls were familiar. He was still sitting askew, studying the buggy, when July and Hassan came up beside him, riding double on her pinto.

"That's Hash Harker's rig, ain't it?" she said.

Jess nodded. "Where's Jacob and Jody?"

"Hoofing it. Their horse run away."

"Jody forgot to hobble it," Hassan said.

"What you reckon Hash wants here?" July asked.

"Look, sis," Jess said. "You want to do me a favor?"

"What'll you gimme?"

"Two rounds."

"Six."

"Unh-ugh."

"Five?"

"No."

"Four?"

"Maybe three."

"Four!"

"Three," he repeated.

She sighed and said, "All right, but only on account of you're my best brother. What you want?"

"You and Hassan wait here. If that buggy ain't left by the time Jacob and Jody come along, you tell them I said they should go on around back real quiet and hole up in the barn till I fetch them. I'll handle Harker."

"What you gonna do, Jesse? You gonna shoot him?"

"Not right now, I don't reckon."

"But you *are* gonna do it, ain't you? When? Can I watch? You won't do it lest I'm there to see, will you, Jesse?"

Hell, he thought. He said, "What you figure I'd want to shoot Hash Harker for?"

"On account of that city ladyfriend of his what

you stopped the coach for and kissed, I reckon. You'd shoot him on account of her, wouldn't you?"

"Not of my own choosing."

July wrinkled her nose and worked her mouth. She spat into the dust. Eyeing Jess, she framed a new thought.

"You gonna beat him up?"

"No."

"Is he gonna beat you up?"

"Hell, no!"

"What *are* you gonna do?"

"Depends," he said significantly.

Hassan nodded in solemn agreement.

July gave another long sad sigh.

"You just stay here, do what I said," Jess told her. "There ain't nothing fancy gonna happen betwixt me and Hash Harker tonight."

July looked askance at him, perhaps disbelieving, perhaps disappointed.

He straightened in the saddle and rode on toward the house. July and Hassan waited, watching as he dismounted and walked up onto the porch. He went to the open parlor window and glanced in before he went inside.

The buggy tied in front of the house rocked a bit, but July failed to notice. Swinging a leg over the pinto's withers, she slid to the ground.

"You wait here, do what Jess said," she told Hassan.

"Why?"

" 'Cause."

"I'm coming, too."

"No, you ain't. You wait here."

"But —"

"You do what Jess said for me, and when I get my bullets, I'll let you shoot my gun," she offered.

He considered, then agreed.

July turned toward the house. But she stopped short and pointed, whispering loudly at Hassan, "Look!"

The looming shadow of the buggy leaned and suddenly lurched. A piece of shadow broke away to become the figure of a man. He skulked toward the porch.

"Who's that?" Hassan asked.

July shook her head. "Dunno. But it's Hash Harker's buggy, and whoever he is, he's been hid in it."

"Uh-huh." That much was obvious.

They saw the man climb onto the porch and sidle up to the open window. As he looked in, light outlined his face.

"It's Hash himself!" July said with a scowl.

"I'll bet he ain't up to no good, sneaking around that way."

"I'll bet he means to bushwhack Jesse on account of that ladyfriend of his!" July hauled her gun from within her dress. Brandishing it, she started for the house. "I'll get him!"

"You ain't got no bullets left," Hassan called after her.

She kept going, hurrying through the darkness. As she neared the porch, she slowed. The man at the window wasn't aware of her, and she meant to keep it that way. Still clutching the gun, she dropped to her hands and knees and crept closer.

Under the house, one of the hounds opened an eye, yawned, and went back to sleep.

Cautiously, July peeked over the edge of the porch. Harker was still crouching at the window. He seemed to be eavesdropping on whatever was happening inside. His hands, resting on the sill, were empty.

Maybe he hadn't come to bushwhack Jesse after all, July thought. Maybe he'd only come to do some spying. That, she could understand. It was one of her own favorite pastimes.

Satisfied that her brother was safe for the time being, she returned her gun to its hiding place and squirmed on around to the side of the house. The parlor window there was well above her head. She rolled a barrel over from the barn, perched on it, and peeked in.

Dominic Johanssen was sitting on the far end of the sofa, away from the place where the gingham had split and the stuffing was spilling out. The saucer he balanced carefully on his knee was the good one that had only a small chip out of the rim. It had been that way already when Deke Wiley traded the tea set off a wagon peddler for a secret Indian mange-salve recipe that he'd made up on the spot.

Dominic was artfully lifting his moustache

with an extended forefinger as he put his cup to his lips when Jess walked in.

January was sitting stiffly in a side chair, holding her teacup in her lap. She hadn't tasted the tea. She'd been doing her best to make polite conversation with Dominic, but it hadn't been easy. From the moment she learned that he wanted to see Jess and that he hadn't brought Junie along to visit with her family, Jan had been certain he carried bad news of some kind. But it wouldn't have been proper for her to ask outright. She was waiting anxiously for Jess to get home so she could find out what was wrong.

Mrs. Deke rested in her rocker in the corner across from her daughter. She sat as she had on the porch, with her hands in her lap folded over her bottle of laudanum. Her head was leaning against the little pillow tied onto the high back of the rocker. Her eyes were almost closed. She was smiling softly to herself. She seemed to have forgotten the guest on the sofa. And if she noticed Jess when he walked in, she showed no sign of it.

Jess nodded to his sister and looked in question at Dominic. " 'Evening, Dom," he said.

Dominic put his teacup on the saucer, took the saucer from his knee, rose, brushed the fringes of his moustache back into place, made a small sociable gesture, and said, " 'Evening, Jesse."

For a moment they just looked at each other. Then Dominic set down the teacup, cleared his throat, and said, "Looks like it's gonna be a nice night."

Jess nodded. "Kinda hot, though."

"Always seems to get that way this time of the year."

"Yeah, it does that."

"Should start to cool off a bit in a couple of months, though."

"Sure hope so."

"Maybe the rain'll come early this year."

"That'd be nice," Mrs. Deke murmured so softly that no one noticed.

"Be a good thing," Jess said. He wondered what Dominic wanted and why it was taking him so long to get to it.

"Grass is awful dry and scant."

"Uh-huh."

"Jesse," Dominic said. He shuffled his feet. His face was mottled with embarrassed red and miserable white. He fingered his moustache again.

"Jesse," he repeated, moving a hand toward the front of his coat. It touched a lapel and halted. "I got . . . I . . . a problem, kinda . . . I — er . . ."

His fingers seemed about to reach for something within the coat. Then they changed their mind and flattened themselves against his chest. Whatever he had intended to say, it wasn't what he said. The words that tumbled out of him were just a stall.

"You heard anything from your Pa yet, Jesse?"

Jess shook his head.

"Been gone awhile now, ain't he?"

"Uh-huh."

"You reckon he'll be back soon?"

"Maybe."

"You don't know just when, though, eh?"

Jess shook his head again. He wished Dom would get on with it, whatever it was. This waiting was beginning to wear on him.

The fingers resting against Dominic's chest stirred as if they'd reconsidered reaching inside the coat. But again they subsided.

Dominic said, "You're expecting to hear from him soon now, eh?"

Jess shrugged.

"Hell, man!" a voice pained with exhausted impatience screeched through the front window. "Get on with it!"

Dominic wheeled toward the window, his hand pressed hard against his chest. The face framed in the window glared at him. He scowled back at it. "Hash! Dammit, you ain't got no business here!"

" 'Evening, Hash," Jess said.

" 'Evening, Jesse," Hash replied. He nodded toward January and Mrs. Deke. " 'Evening, ladies."

" 'Evening, Mr. Harker," January said.

Mrs. Deke didn't seem to notice the greeting. She was smiling to herself about whatever she was seeing behind her closed eyelids.

"Hash, you ain't got no business here,"

Dominic said again.

"I sure have. It's *my* affair, ain't it? It's *my* note you come to deliver, ain't it?"

"Oh," Jess said, understanding.

"What note?" January asked.

Nobody answered her.

Dominic gave Harker a grudging nod of agreement, but said, "It ain't right, though. You ain't supposed to be here."

"Why not?"

"I told you. It's in the book."

"What book?" January asked.

Again, she got no answer.

Dominic waved a hand wildly at Harker. "Get me the book, just get me the book! I'll show you!"

Louder, January repeated, "What book?"

This time she got Dominic's attention.

"Book of rules. It's right out in the buggy." He turned to Harker again. "Get it, and I'll show you! It says you ain't supposed to be here!"

Harker's face disappeared from the window.

Inside the parlor, January tugged at her brother's sleeve and asked, "Please, Jesse, what's this all about?"

Jess looked to Dominic. "You brung me something?"

"A note." Dominic slapped his chest just above the inside coat pocket. Then his fingers dived into the pocket. They came out with a carefully folded sheet of paper sealed with a glob of dark red wax. "Here!"

Jess took it gingerly. He broke the seal, thumbed it open, and handed it back to Dominic.

"What is it?" January asked.

"Challenge," Dominic said. He squinted at it, then began to read aloud.

"To Jesse Wiley. My Dear Sir: Whereas upon this very day the addressee, one Jesse Wiley of Hardly, Texas, has duly caused grievous insult to one Miss Lucinda Cummins of Fairwater, Virginia, I, the undersigned, do, in this lady's behalf, hereby challenge the above addressee to settle this matter of honor in an honorable manner, in such appropriate place, at such appropriate time, in such appropriate way, with such appropriate weapons, as may be agreed upon by the bearer of this message and such friend as the above addressee may deem appropriate, in keeping with honorable custom among gentlemen. A reply at the earliest possible convenience is humbly requested by, Most Sincerely Your Humble Obedient Servant, H. Harker, Esq. P.S. Nothing less than blood will be appropriate to satisfy such an insult. YHOS."

January frowned at the paper. "What's all that supposed to mean?"

"A duel!" July hollered through the window. "Jesse and Hash are gonna fight a duel!"

CHAPTER 8

Hassan followed July's instructions to the letter. He waited until Jacob and Jody came struggling along afoot. Keeping his distance from them, he told them that Jess had said for them to go on around back real quiet and hole up in the barn till Jess fetched them. Then, before either one could grab his mount away from him, he hightailed it.

He swung wide around the house and left the pony in the Wileys' corral. Then he hurried to join July. He got there just as she shouted, "A duel!"

As he climbed up onto the barrel stand beside him, she threw her arms around him. The gesture was pure excitement. The act was pure pleasure. For a moment, both of them were distracted from the proceedings in the parlor.

But then boards creaked on the porch, calling their attention back into the room.

Hash Harker shoved aside a tatter of curtain to poke his head and one arm through the front window. He held out a small slim book. "Here!"

Dominic grabbed it. He held it up in front of Harker's face and prodded a forefinger at the cover. "See this?"

It was so close that Harker's eyes crossed as he

looked at it. He nodded.

Dominic read it aloud anyway. "*The Code of Honor, or Rules for the Government of Principals and Seconds in Dueling*, by John Lyde Wilson, Savannah, Morning News Steam Press, 1870."

He paused and looked around triumphantly, as if he had irrefutably proven his point.

"All afternoon, I been studying this book," he said. "I been finding out the right way to do this here thing. It's got to be done *right*. You-all understand that?"

Heads bobbed uncertainly.

Something tugged on July's dress. She pivoted and found herself glowering at Jacob and Jody. Jacob still had a hand on her skirt.

"You let go of me," she growled.

"What's going on?" Jacob said.

"Plenty."

"What?"

"You'd like to know, wouldn't you?"

Jacob tugged her skirt again. Harder this time. It was a threat. He'd pull her off the barrel if she didn't tell him.

She tightened her grip on Hassan. She'd half a mind never to tell Jacob what was happening. But it was too good a secret to keep to herself. "All right. Hash Harker's done went and challenged Jesse to a duel."

Jacob's eyes widened. "The hell! A duel? With guns?"

July supposed they'd use guns. As much as she liked the idea, she couldn't quite imagine her brother going after Harker with a sword. Jesse didn't even own a sword. She didn't know anybody who did.

Jody poked Jacob in the ribs. "That'll sure be all the talk, won't it? Our own brother and Hash Harker fighting a real-live duel with each other!"

A grin spread itself across Jacob's face. "It sure will. It'll be the biggest thing has happened around Hardly since Big Jim Boohm left town."

He pulled on July's skirt again. "Make some room. Lemme see."

She kicked him in the shoulder and said, "Go find your own place to watch from."

Jody would have fought her for the window, but Jacob had an idea. "Come on, boy. We can watch from inside. We got no need to peek through windows like young'uns."

"But Jesse left word we wasn't to come inside till he told us," Jody said.

"The hell with that. I'm gonna watch through the hall door." Jacob started toward the rear of the house.

Jody hurried along after him.

Inside the parlor, Dominic had been reading from the little book. His finger traced along the first page of text as he spoke. When it reached bottom, he looked up and said, "You know what that means?"

Harker nodded. Jess and January looked on blankly.

"It means the principal — that's you, Hash — ain't supposed to even *resent* the insult in public.

You done wrong challenging Jesse yourself, right out in front of everybody. That can't be undone now, but there ain't no reason to go on doing everything wrong. We got the book, and we know what's right. It *ain't* right for you to be here now."

"What's so awful wrong about I just watch through the window?" Harker asked.

"Because on account of you won't keep your mouth shut, for one thing," Dominic told him. "You ain't supposed to so much as *talk* to nobody but your second — that's me — about it all."

"I ain't talking. I only come to listen."

"You ain't supposed to take *no* part in it *no* more until the shooting. I'm your second, and it says you're supposed to leave everything to *my* judgment."

Harker turned to Jess. "You got yourself a second yet?"

"No."

"Got a notion who you want?"

Jess glanced at his twin sister. He wondered if there was any rule against a woman being a second. But before he could ask, the parlor door was swinging wide.

Jacob strode in. Puffing his chest out proudly, he said, "*I'll* be second for Jesse."

Jody followed him in and offered, "I'll third."

"Me, too!" July hollered from her perch at the window.

"No!" Dominic shouted.

Jacob scowled at him. "Why not?"

"It can't be no blood kin."

"Not even my own brother?" Jess asked.

Dominic shook his head.

"Like hell!" Jacob bellowed. "I ain't gonna get left out of this. I'm gonna be a second."

"Me, too," Jody said.

July decided to watch them fight it out among themselves before she moved in and took over.

Dominic kept shaking his head. "It says in the book a man's second can't be no son, nor father, nor brother."

"That's a funny sort of rule," January said. "Seems like a man's blood kin ought to be the ones to stand up beside him in such a thing."

"Well, they ain't," Dominic told her.

"Why not?" Jess asked.

" 'Cause it says so in the book!" Dominic's voice was getting louder. The red mottling was spreading over his face. "Can't none of you to hell understand? *It says so in the book!*"

"Ain't no damn book telling *me* what I can't do," Jacob said.

Jody nodded agreement.

"What about it, Hash?" Jess said. "You mind if Jacob stands for me?"

"Far as I'm concerned, you can have whoever you want," Harker said sociably.

"But he can't!" Dominic insisted.

"It's all right with me," Harker said.

Dominic made a sort of strangling noise. His face was turning solid red. His mouth gaped and spilled out words. "I should of knowed it was wrong for me to let you rope me into this thing. I should of knowed it was wrong to let you drive me out here to do it. I should of knowed you wouldn't never stay put in the buggy like you promised. I should of drove myself —"

"I don't let nobody but me drive my Messenger-bred trotter."

"I could of drove myself in my own rig. That's what I should of done. I only had to come give Jesse that fool note and leave again. That's all." Dominic turned to Jess. "I only just had to give you the note and say as how you had to get yourself a second and have him see me to set things up. That's all. From then on it'd be betwixt me and him, without Hash nor you having a word on it. That ain't nothing Hash has to break the rules so he could come watch for, is it?"

Jess shrugged.

"I ain't doing no harm being here," Harker said.

The creak of Mrs. Deke's rocker stopped. She cleared her throat.

In sudden silence, everyone turned to look at her.

Her eyes were halfway open. She peered at the front window. "Was that Mr. Harker's voice I heard?"

Harker gave a quick, polite little nod of his head toward her. "Yes, ma'am."

"Jesse," she said slowly. "Why don't you invite Mr. Harker inside? January, fetch another cup of tea for our guest."

Harker started to swing a leg over the window-sill.

"You can't come in here," Dominic protested. "You ain't supposed to be here at all."

"Hell," Harker answered, setting a foot on the floor. "I got some rights, ain't I? It's *my* duel, ain't it?"

Jacob stretched himself up to his full height. He glowered at Dominic. "*I* say I'm gonna second for my brother. Ain't nobody gonna cheat me out of being in on this."

"No! It can't be no blood kin," Dominic answered.

"Hash says it's all right, and it is his duel," Jess said.

Harker pulled his other leg over the windowsill and stood up. He nodded agreement.

"No," Dominic said. The book was still open in his hands. He slapped it closed and slammed it down on the table. "No! I ain't gonna do it! I didn't want to in the first place, only Junie asked me to. I only done it at all because she wanted me to."

"Done what because Junie wanted it?" Jess asked.

Dominic hooked a thumb toward Harker. "I agreed to come be second for him on account of Junie's all calf-eyed over him and she wanted me to. But there's limits to what a man can do, even for a woman. I swear, there's limits!"

With that, he wheeled and stalked out of the room.

"Come back, Dom!" Harker called. "I'll do it your way if that's what Junie wants!"

But Dominic had made his decision. He tromped out onto the porch. The planks squeaked in rhythm to his determined steps. He thundered down the stairs. A bit chain rattled. Well-greased axles complained softly as wheels began to turn. Hooves thudded on hard-packed earth.

"Hell," Harker muttered, frowning to himself. "What am I gonna do for a second?"

Jacob cocked his head and eyed him. "If my little sister Junie wants you to have a second, you got one."

"Who?"

"Me."

"Huh?"

"Uh-huh." Jacob nodded solemnly. "If it's what Junie wants, *I'll* do it."

Mrs. Deke spoke suddenly. "Jacob? Is that you, Jacob?"

"Yes'm."

"Is Jody here, too?"

"Yes'm." The boy stepped forward.

"What about July? I thought I heard July."

"I'm here, Ma," July called as she clambered in through the window.

Hassan started to follow her, then changed his mind. Leaning his elbows on the sill, he watched from outside.

Mrs. Deke's eyes shifted under their heavy lids. Fondly she said, "All my young'uns."

"All except Junie," Jess told her.

"Junie," she murmured. After a moment of thought, she said, "Junie's went away."

"She moved to town," January said.

Mrs. Deke blinked. Her eyelids returned to their half-open position. The pupils under them were dark and liquid. They seemed to be looking at something very far away.

After a moment she spoke again. "Mr. Wiley's dead."

Jess's jaw dropped. He stared at his mother. Jacob and Jody stared at each other. Hash Harker stared down at his own feet. January hurried to her mother's side.

July frowned and asked, "What you mean, Ma?"

"Mr. Wiley. You know. Your Pa. He's dead," Mrs. Deke replied. Her rocker creaked in agreement.

"I . . . I . . ." Harker glanced around at the Wileys. "I had no idea. I wouldn't never of intruded with such unpleasant business if I . . . I . . ." He settled his gaze on Jess. "I'd of waited until tomorrow. Believe me. It's downright ungentlemanly. I wouldn't never of done it intentionally."

He turned to Mrs. Deke and bowed deep from the waist. "Ma'am, please accept my condolences and apologies."

She smiled faintly at him. "It was nice of you to call . . ." She paused, trying to remember his name. She was certain she'd known it a moment ago, but now it refused to come to her. She decided it didn't matter. Her eyelids drooped.

"Such a nice young man," she murmured.

"Please do call again, Mr. Harker," January said dutifully. She moved toward the door, intending to politely see him out.

"I can find my own way." He bowed again, this time to January. "Thank you for your hospitality, Miss Wiley."

There was a moment of silence while he disappeared through the doorway. Once he was gone, Jody turned to Jacob and asked, "What happened to Pa?"

Jacob leaned toward his mother. "What happened to Pa, Ma?"

"He's dead."

Jess asked, "You got a message?"

"I didn't see any messenger," January told him.

"I got a *feeling*." Mrs. Deke said. "It come to me."

Jess looked to his twin sister. She met his eyes and nodded. They shared a common thought. January voiced it.

"She's got a natural way for them feelings."

The others nodded, all solemn-faced and awed.

Mrs. Deke spoke up again. "Don't you young'uns go concerning yourselves. He'll be back 'fore long."

"But if he's dead —" Jess began.

She interrupted him. "I know. But he'll be back."

July had been searching through her clothing as if she were after a particularly fast and active rabbit. Coming up with her revolver, she demanded, "Who killed him?"

"Hush," January said.

"I'll get 'em!" She waved the gun toward each brother in turn. "Gimme some ammunition! I'll leave right now. Better gimme twenty, thirty rounds. I ain't such a good shot, you know. But I'll get 'em!"

"You hold on," Jess said. "Everybody hold on. If something really has happened to Pa, we'll get the word right quick. Else he'll be back soon himself to tell us different."

"He'll be back." Mrs. Deke sounded certain of it. Her eyes were closed again. She was smiling contentedly to herself as she rocked.

The porch creaked suddenly. Someone rapped at the window.

"Huh?" Jess called.

Hash Harker poked his head through. He looked sorely embarrassed.

"Begging your pardon," he said. "I truly do hate to intrude again at a time like this, but I sort of — uh — I wonder, could I maybe borrow the lend of a mount for the night. I — uh — Dom's went and took off with my buggy and horse."

"Not that Messenger-bred trotting horse you don't let nobody but you drive?" Jacob asked.

Harker sighed morosely and nodded. "This just ain't been a good day for me," he said.

CHAPTER 9

The morning sun streaked the yard of the Wiley place with long shadows. In the corral, the using horses munched noisily at the hay Jess had forked out for them first thing. Under the house, the hounds stirred and scratched at early-rising fleas. Around the open doors of the kitchen, the chickens chuckled over food scraps January had tossed out. In the rear bedroom Jody, who'd sneaked back after his early-morning chores, lay snoring softly to himself. In the larger pecan tree, the vulture stretched its wings and yawned. On the porch, Mrs. Deke rocked slowly. The monotonous squeak of her rocker stopped momentarily as she sipped from her laudanum bottle, then started up again.

Mrs. Deke was sitting with her back to the sun and her hands folded over the bottle in her lap. Through half-closed eyes she contemplated the fat fly-specked German wurst hanging from the post at the far end of the porch.

Mr. Wiley had a fondness for sausages. Junie had sent this one in from town for him several days ago. Mrs. Deke wasn't sure how many days it had been, but since Mr. Wiley wasn't back home yet, the sausage still hung there, waiting

95

and ripening. She had a notion it was plenty ripe now, and if he wanted it, he'd better come get it soon.

Through the fringes of her eyelids she noticed something among the leaves of the pecan. Great black wings spread out. A huge shadow rose from the tree. She blinked and saw the shadow swoop and come skimming across the yard toward her.

The vulture was aimed at the porch. Its path would take it in under the roof. As it passed the end post, it snatched the wurst with its talons. A cloud of flies buzzed curses as it swept the sausage away from them.

The sausage was tied to a nail in the post. The string jerked back before it snapped. The sausage escaped the vulture's grip. It hit the floor, bounced twice, and rolled, coming to rest about a handspan short of falling off the porch. A fly instantly lit on it.

The vulture let out a squawk. Turning sharply, it swung back toward the end of the porch. It landed with a grunt. Tottering, it planted one set of talons possessively on the sausage. The fly left.

With its wings half-furled, the vulture cocked its head and stared at Mrs. Deke through one shiny, squinty eye.

She stared back at it. She saw its squint, the tough red wrinkled hide of its bald head, and its scrawny neck, and the sharp-hooked beak, with a sense of familiarity.

A *feeling* surged through her.

Her face opened into a broad grin. Joy filled her voice.

"Mr. Wiley! You're back! I knowed you'd come back soon!"

The vulture bobbed its head and took a bite out of the sausage.

The outbuildings on the Wiley place were mostly built from the same green lumber as the house. The barn was nothing fancy, just a shed with a hayloft. The planks of its walls, like those of the house, had warped and shrunk and dropped out knots. The breeze wafting through them this morning carried two strange sounds. First came a flapping like huge wings, then the voice of Mrs. Deke.

During the past few years Mrs. Deke had rarely spoken loud enough to be heard more than a few paces away. At the sound of her mother's voice reaching all the way into the loft, July frowned in puzzlement. Rising to her knees, she peered at the house through a knothole.

"What's the matter?" Hassan asked her.

"It's Ma." Her tone was hushed with awe. "There's a big old turkey buzzard setting on the porch with her, and she's talking to it."

Hassan scrambled to his knees and scuttled to her side. He peeked out through a crack in the wall. "I bet that's the same buzzard."

"The one Jesse wanted me to kill?" July reached for her gun. It seemed to have slipped out of its usual hiding place. Patting her dress in search of it, she said, "I'll get that old bird. I'll . . . Oh-oh . . ."

"What?"

"I shot up all my cartridges on that rabbit we et yesterday. I'll get more, though." Her head almost brushed the rafters as she stood up. Ducking a little, she started for the ladder.

Hassan hurried after her as far as the doorway of the barn. He halted there. Staying in the shadows, he watched her stride toward the house.

Jody's bunk was in the rear bedroom of the house. He lay sprawled flat on his back in it, with his arms spread wide and his spurred boots hanging over the end. He was dreaming about a woman. No particular woman. Any woman.

He stopped snoring suddenly.

"Ma?" he mumbled.

He wasn't sure whether he'd heard his mother's voice, or only dreamed it. Whichever it was, he wished it hadn't interrupted him right when it did. He felt a downright desperate need to finish out the dream he'd been having. He hoped he'd be able to pick it up again.

Yawning, he sat up and stretched and looked at the back window. It opened onto the porch a little behind where his Ma usually sat in her rocker. He walked stiffly over and leaned out.

Wincing, he jerked back.

There was a monstrous big buzzard setting on

the far end of the porch, staring at his Ma.

Or was there?

It seemed awful unlikely. Maybe it was a piece of a dream, too. He gave his head a shake and rubbed his eyes. Then, resting his hands on the windowsill, he tilted forward again, very slowly this time. The back of his Ma's rocker came into view first. Beyond it, the big black bird appeared.

Jody blinked.

It didn't go away.

He blinked again, and decided that it was really real. And it seemed to be paying a neighborly social call on his Ma.

Turning, he went to Jacob's bunk and began to hunt through the bedding. He had just decided that what he needed right now was a good hearty jolt of hard whiskey.

Jacob had ridden home with Hash Harker to work out details of the forthcoming duel. He'd stayed the night at Harker's. In fact, after being properly introduced to Miss Lucinda Cummins of Fairwater, Virginia, he had decided that he really ought to stay on at Harker's at least until the duel was over.

Since Miss Cummins and her chaperon, Mrs. Quick, had the guest room, Jacob had made do with the big fancy sofa in Harker's company parlor. Sleeping late, he dreamed of a buzzard. But that didn't seem at all unusual to him. He liked buzzards and dreamed of them often.

Jess had finished up his before-breakfast chores, and January had assured him there was plenty of time before she'd be setting food on the table, so he'd saddled up the little black filly that his Pa had brought back from the last trip to Mexico.

The filly was a neat little animal with big liquid eyes and ways as sociable as a house pet. She was well-mannered under a saddle, but she had only been trained to a hackamore. Jess figured that, properly broken to a bit, she'd bring a good price as a ladies' mount. Whenever he'd had the time and inclination, he'd been riding her out and gently working her to the iron.

This morning he slipped a headstall with a low-ported bit over her hackamore and rode out to work her awhile before breakfast. When the buzzard flapped down to help itself to the sausage, he was out of sight and earshot. He never heard Mrs. Deke call out to the bird.

The kitchen shed wasn't far from the back porch. January had both its doors open. During the summer, with the huge iron range going full blast, even that didn't help much. The kitchen was nigh unbearable.

Usually at this time of year January wouldn't stoke up the ovens. She let her family make do with pan breads. But this morning, because of the impending duel, she'd decided to make up a little nicey or two especially for Jess.

January felt a powerful tenderness toward her

twin brother, and she was downright fearful about the duel. Hash Harker was a good hand with a gun. She wouldn't mind so much if Jess got hurt only a bit. Then she could devote herself to nursing him back to health. But she was almost distraught over the possibility that he could get killed.

She thought her fear was all for her brother. She had no idea of the futile emptiness she would have felt if Jess hadn't been there for her to cluck over and look after and worry for.

This morning she had mixed up a batch of biscuits and a couple of pies to go along with the usual pot of beans and slabs of fry and cornmeal pan bread. It had meant a lot of fussing around in the kitchen, a lot of suffering in the intense heat, but she'd told herself it was all worthwhile if it meant Jess would have a nice breakfast. She was completely unaware of how thoroughly she enjoyed suffering for the sake of her family, and for her twin brother in particular.

Sweat-soaked hair was straggling limply around her face, and streaks of sweat were rolling down her cheeks to drip from her chin as she sneaked a quick look into the oven. She was swabbing at her face with a corner of her apron when she heard her mother's voice.

Puzzled, she wiped her hands on her apron and started out. She stopped short in the doorway.

The hulking black figure of a huge turkey buzzard was perched on the end of the porch. And it had stolen Pa's sausage.

Her first impulse was to run shooing it as if it were a recalcitrant chicken. Then she remembered the buzzard that had been plaguing Jess yesterday. It looked like the same bird. Jess had thought it might be an omen of some kind.

Now here it was sitting on the porch, staring at her Ma as if it were the Angel of Death come to fetch Mrs. Deke away. Or maybe to bring disaster down onto the whole Wiley family.

The three of them were converging toward the porch at once: Jody with his throat still stinging from Jacob's whiskey, and the mists of dreams still clinging to the corners of his thoughts; July with her hand pressed against the empty gun hidden under her dress, and her mind on the cartridges she might get from her brothers' revolvers, if she could find them; and January clutching her apron, feeling chilled with dimly delicious apprehension.

Mrs. Deke was aware of them. Raising her voice again, she called out happily, "Young'uns, your Pa's come home."

The vulture had the sausage pinned down and had already bitten several good-sized chunks out of it. Looking up, the glowering black bird pivoted its head. Wrinkles twisted into its scrawny neck as it scanned the Wileys. It opened its beak wide and made a soft chuckling sound. Then, with a quick darting motion, it took another bite out of the sausage.

"I told you he'd come," Mrs. Deke said.

Jody sidled up to his mother, his eyes still on the buzzard. Crouching, he asked, "Where is Pa? He didn't bring that *thing* back with him, did he?"

Mrs. Deke's smile was gentle and warm. Her head moved slightly, a faint suggestion of a nod toward the buzzard.

"There he is."

"Huh?"

Jody stared at the bird. So did January and July. It cocked its head and returned their gazes with one imperturbable bright eye.

"That thing?" July said. "My Pa?"

"Being dead wouldn't never stop Mr. Wiley from coming back home," Mrs. Deke murmured. "I knowed it wouldn't."

"You ain't trying to say he's went and come back as a buzzard?" July asked.

Jody studied the bird. Tentatively, he admitted, "It does kinda look like Pa."

January gave a wavery nod. She was sure the bird was an omen of some kind. She wondered if her mother might not be right. With that leathery old face and that squinty look to its eye, the buzzard really did bear a strong likeness to Deke Wiley.

Hesitantly she whispered, "Maybe it is Pa."

July's eyes were wide and glistening with excitement. She'd never anywhere ever heard of anyone having a buzzard for a father. Not even all the strange books Hassan had told her about mentioned such a thing.

A skeptical doubt reared itself up in her mind. She gave it a good hefty mental kick, and nodded in solemn agreement with her sister.

Jody's mouth felt dry clear down to his gullet. He wished he'd brought Jacob's bottle along with him. This was an awful lot for a man to cope with all at once without a drink. He thought about how the girls in town ragged him now over something as ordinary as his being young. What were they going to say when they found out his Pa had turned into a buzzard? He sure wished Jacob was on hand to advise him.

CHAPTER 10

They were all talking together, all intent on their conversation, except Mrs. Deke. She was intent on the buzzard. She sat rocking slowly, smiling at it.

The bird swiveled its head to peer toward the sounds of approaching hoofbeats.

"What is it, Mr. Wiley?" Mrs. Deke asked.

The others stopped their talk and turned to look. Jody spotted the rider on the black filly coming toward the house.

"Looks like Jesse yonder," he said, pointing.

July glowered at him. She resented it when he got in ahead of her on anything. She said, "Of course. Who'd you expect?"

He hadn't expected anybody. He hadn't even known Jess was away from the house. He stuck his tongue out at her.

January gasped, "My biscuits!"

Clutching the hem of her apron, she dashed toward the kitchen. The breeze was wafting thin smudges of smoke through the open doors.

The vulture helped itself to another bite of sausage.

Jess enjoyed working out the filly. He would

have liked to ride longer, maybe all morning. But there were things he had to do today. And he was expected home in time for breakfast.

Topping a rise, he saw the house, and the large dark object on the back porch.

For an instant he thought it might be his Pa all rigged up in black. That was a color Deke Wiley favored, especially for working clothes. But then Jess realized the thing hadn't the shape of a man.

It could still mean his Pa was back, though. It might be some hulking black hunk of trade goods he'd brought up from Mexico with him. Nobody ever knew what Deke Wiley was likely to drag in.

Then Jess recognized the thing on the end of the porch for what it was.

Something as chilly as sleet trickled down inside his spine. Just as certain as if it wore a brand, he knew this was the same damn buzzard. And he felt sure now that it was an omen.

The filly reared, snorting at the sudden jerk of the bit against the tender bars of her mouth.

Settling her, patting her withers to steady her, Jess mumbled a curse at himself. He'd jerked the reins as he flinched at his own thoughts. And those thoughts, he told himself, were plain foolishness. Buzzards were plenty common in these parts. Just because one chose this morning to sit on the back porch was no proof it was an omen come to threaten him. Was it?

Keeping the filly to a slow lope, he rode on toward the house. He held the pace as he reached the yard.

The vulture twisted its head full around to stare at him. He refused to meet its squinting eye.

"Jesse!" Jody called to him.

He didn't answer, but rode on to the corral and dismounted at the gate.

July jumped off the porch and ran toward him. Without giving her so much as a glance, he pulled the headstall off the filly, then hooked the nigh stirrup over the saddle horn and loosed the girth.

"Jesse! You'll never guess what!" July said.

"Ain't interested in guessing what," he grunted. He dragged the saddle off the filly's back and flung it over the top corral rail.

"You see that buzzard on the porch?" she tried, in hope of rousing his interest.

Ignoring her, he opened the gate and turned the filly into the corral.

July scowled at her brother. He'd got right stubborn all of a sudden. She had half a mind not to tell him what had happened. But if she didn't, Jody would. She couldn't let Jody have that privilege.

"Pa's come back," she announced.

Jess looked at her. "Where is he?"

"On the porch." She waved a hand toward the vulture.

"Huh?"

"There!" She pointed directly at the bird.

Jess saw his mother in her rocker, and Jody on the steps, and that damn buzzard. No one else. He turned back to July.

"It ain't *my* idea," she told him. "Ma's the one who said it. She says Pa's up and died and now he's come back as that there old turkey buzzard."

"Like hell," Jess muttered. He squinted at the bird. It squinted back at him. A part of his mind whispered that it was just the kind of thing Deke Wiley would do. Another part whispered that it was all a lot of foolishness.

"It's true," July insisted.

Jody came tromping up with an air of importance and said, "Jesse, Ma wants to see you."

"I reckon," Jess said. He glanced back at the filly. She was down rubbing her saddle-sweaty back in the sand. He wished he were still aboard her, still somewhere out in the *llano,* riding hard, not heading back this way at all.

"It's the same buzzard," July was saying. "The one you wanted me to shoot. What if I'd shot it, Jesse? What if I'd up and shot my own Pa?"

Jess wished she'd shut up.

Then Jody began saying something about the buzzard.

Jess wished they'd both shut up. With his mouth set, he strode across the yard toward the porch.

As he reached the bottom step, January came out of the kitchen. Using her apron for a potholder, she held out a baking sheet with rows of hard black cinders spaced out neatly on it. Small wisps of smoke curled from them. She thrust them in front of Jess.

Her eyes were moist, her cheeks red from the heat of the kitchen. Her face was as mournful sad as if she brought news of a massacre. "Jesse, I'd meant you a real fine breakfast, but I reckon I burnt the biscuits."

He glanced down at them. "I reckon."

"I kinda overcooked the pies, too," she confessed. "But they ain't quite so bad. If you scrape the black off the top, the innards'll be all right, I think."

"Uh-huh."

She thought he didn't sound like he cared. All her work and suffering gone to ashes, and now Jess just plain didn't care. None of them ever really appreciated what she went through for them.

Two fat tears formed on her lashes. Breaking loose, they rolled down her cheeks. They mingled with the sweat, indistinguishable from it. Looking into her face, Jess was completely unaware of them.

He asked, "Sis, what's all this about that buzzard?"

She snuffled, then said, "Ma says it's Pa."

"What do you think?"

She thought that on a horrible day like this, when everything was going all wrong, there was a good chance that the big black bird really was her father.

She said, "I reckon she's right."

Jess shook his head in denial.

That was too much for January. After all of the trouble and misery he had caused her by giving her a reason to fix up a whopping fine breakfast for him, now he was disagreeing with her. All her doubts about the buzzard vanished in a puff of anger.

"You don't know, Jesse Wiley! You just plain don't know nothing at all! That there buzzard is our Pa, all right, and he's dead, and he's come back here like that as an omen to us that there's gonna be more dying! I know. I got a *feeling* like Ma gets. There's gonna be blood and misery and all kinds of awful things!"

July and Jody gaped wide-eyed at their sister. Neither of them had imagined the vulture meant anything quite like that.

"Hold on, sis," Jess said.

But January had no intention of holding on. She'd built up a good flow of tears, and she intended to make the most of them. Bowing her head, she pressed her face into her hands and sobbed.

"It ain't that bad," Jess insisted, though he wasn't at all sure it wasn't. But he figured it was his duty to comfort his sister. "Looky here, everybody's got all strung out and shaky. Let's us set down quiet to breakfast and rest ourselves. Once we've et, we'll all feel better."

"We . . . we . . ." January whimpered through her fingers.

Suddenly she jerked up her head, a whole new thought in her eyes. "The fry! I left it on the stove!"

Grabbing her skirts, she ran toward the kitchen. Jess raced after her. Smoke was roiling through the open doors.

They managed to get the fire out before it could take hold on the walls or the roof, and after a while the breeze cleared the smoke out enough for January to set up a new pan of meat.

The breakfast didn't help at all. The beans, the pies, and the biscuits were all burnt past bearability. As if to make up for the overcooking, January had taken the fresh fry and the corn-bread off the fire too soon. The slices of salted hog meat tasted like warmed-up lard, and the pone had the flavor of chicken feed.

Jody begged off eating altogether, claiming he felt a little sick to the stomach. After a good look at that breakfast, he actually did.

To prove her superiority to Jody, July struggled through several mouthfuls of the stuff. But then she gave up and left. She and Hassan ate raw eggs from under the brooding hen, then collected the pinto and rode off a ways to watch the house from hiding. They knew Jess would be going into town to find himself a second for the duel. They meant to trail after him and find out what happened. And, incidentally, to scrounge up something more to eat.

For the sake of January's feelings, Jess stuck it

out at the table, eating as much as he could stand. But his efforts didn't seem to cheer her. She just sat there with her head hung down and her shoulders occasionally heaving from a particularly deep sob. She never touched the food, or lifted her eyes toward Jess. She didn't do anything except sit there suffering.

Finally Jess couldn't take it any longer. He shoved away from the table and stalked out to catch himself a horse.

Jody had left for town to hunt up a decent meal. He was off down the road, almost out of sight, when Jess came slamming out of the house. Jess waited until he was clear out of sight, and then some, before putting his spurs to the roan's flanks.

January stayed on at the table. She hoped Jess would come back in and discover her sitting there. Then maybe he'd appreciate how much she went through for his sake.

When she heard the roan leaving the yard, she knew it was too late. With a sigh, she gave up her crying and began to gather the dishes.

There was plenty of garbage this morning. She dumped it in the yard and hollered for the hounds. She didn't have to call the chickens. They'd been standing by expectantly.

It took the old hounds awhile to stir from under the house. Bugler waddled out first, sniffed, and sat down to scratch his off ear. Bessie followed him, her flabby dugs swaying with every step. Nosing into the garbage, she nuzzled a damp chunk of burnt pie and turned away. Last of all, Old Blue shuffled from under the house, blinking his rheumy eyes. He'd lost his sense of smell years ago, and his sight was failing. It took him awhile to locate the garbage. Finally he found it and began gumming morosely at a piece of overcooked pone.

Bony was the youngest of Deke Wiley's hounds. He had wakened early, roused himself, and set off hunting. While the others were at home rooting through the garbage with small hope of finding anything worth their while, he had licked up a tasty trail of ants and was down the road rolling ecstatically in the decaying carcass of a long-dead crow.

Riding double on the pinto, July and Hassan set out for town. The dogs paid them no mind. But as they passed the seep hole, headed for the wagon road, the vulture rose from its perch on the end of the porch. With a flapping that spooked the chickens and stirred a small show of interest from the hounds, it took off. By the time the hounds had managed to spot the cause of the alarm, the vulture had swung around past the pecan trees and was heading rapidly away. The dogs returned to their rooting through the garbage.

Mrs. Deke had been creaking slowly to and fro in her rocker. Her eyes had been closed, her head filled with soft thoughts. At the sound of the great wings and the clatter of the frightened chickens, she opened them enough to see the big black bird skimming across the yard.

She was sorry to see Mr. Wiley leaving again so soon when he'd just got back from such a long trip. She hoped he wouldn't be gone too far or too long this time.

It seemed odd to her that he hadn't told her where he was going this time. From the look of his path, though, he might only be heading into town. That seemed likely to her. Mr. Wiley was probably eager to have a few drinks with his friends and catch up on the news and, most important of all, make his play in his running checkers game with Whisk Shaker. She figured he'd likely be back by nightfall.

Dimly she recollected something was supposed to be happening tonight. She wasn't sure what. She decided that if it was to involve her, then somebody would likely mention it to her. If it didn't involve her, well, then, it didn't really matter anyway.

As long as she had her eyes open, she thought it might be worthwhile to take another sip of her laudanum. She trickled a slow swallow down her gullet, returned the bottle to her lap, and let her eyelids droop shut again.

CHAPTER 11

The town of Hardly had barely begun to stir itself when Jody arrived on Main Street, but there was one assuring sign of life. A rich aroma of crisping bacon and boiling grits spilled out of Mrs. Grandly's Family Boardinghouse (fifty cents a night, five dollars a week, individual meals twenty-five cents, baths extra). Jody breathed deep, determined the source of the scents, and made an instant decision. Dropping rein at the hitch rail, he hurried into the boardinghouse.

By the time Jess reached Main Street, there was somewhat more activity. McDonald Dudley was out daubing fresh mud into a crack in the Boohm Building. Juan Orlando was slapping at the dust on the decaying plank walk in front of the Boston Emporium with a worn-out straw broom. Matt Matthews was propping open the door of the Gentlemen's Exclusive Tonsorial Parlor with an old buggy anchor. And while assorted dogs were still sleeping in the long morning shadows, several hogs were out hunting food and a pair of dominicker hens were pecking through the fresh droppings just aft of Jody's horse.

But the big front door of the tiny Grand Palace of the Golden Dragon was still closed, and instead of auguring across the table inside by the window, the Reverend P. Jonathan Seven and Ezekiel W. Trot were engrossed in conversation on the bench in front of the saloon.

"Pomegranate," Ezekiel W. Trot said.

"Apple," the Reverend P. Jonathan Seven answered.

Ezekiel was determined. "Pomegranate."

The Reverend was equally determined. "Apple."

"Pomegranate," Ezekiel insisted.

"Apple."

"Pomegranate!"

"Apple!"

Neither of them noticed Jess when he drew rein in front of them. Leaving the roan hitched, he walked around to the back of the building, used the outhouse, then tried the back door of the saloon. It was shut and barred. Hammering his fist against it only made his hand sore.

He stepped back, scooped up a handful of gravel, and flung it at an upstairs window. The window was open. He could hear the gravel shower in onto the floor.

He waited a moment, then tried again. Still no response. He tried a handful of pebbles.

The clatter of stones falling on the floor inside was followed by a creaking and a groaning. A face appeared in the window. It was smeared with Professor Bonneville's Magnolia Oil Complexion Cream, and crowned with a prickly mass of red-rag curlers.

"Nance?" Jess asked.

"Jesse Wiley! Of all . . . What you want here at this Samforsaken hour?"

"Can I come up for a while?"

"No."

"Please. Just to set awhile."

"No."

"I just want to set, maybe talk a little."

"Jesse, I got to have my sleep," the girl said. She turned away from the window and disappeared.

Jess stood staring up at the empty space where the face had been. He heard a faint creak of floorboards and after a moment a sound like a saw. Sighing, he tucked his thumbs into his pockets and strode back to Main Street.

A bit of breeze was ruffling the old-fashioned red and white ribbons that hung from a pole in front of the tonsorial parlor. They caught his eye.

He rubbed the heel of his hand across his chin. His whiskers felt long enough to pass for a young beard instead of simple negligence. He thought maybe he ought to have them cropped for the partying tonight. Maybe indulge in a bath, too. Maybe even get himself a new shirt.

After all, this affair would be a big one, with folks coming in from counties all around. Hash Harker was throwing it to introduce his bride-to-be, and he'd invited everybody.

Returning his thumbs to his pockets, Jess headed for the Gen. Mdse.

McDonald Dudley leaned his elbows on a counter and mused in the lonely silence of his store. The urge to talk, to pass some time sociably in the company of somebody — anybody — welled within him. At the sight of Jess, it burst forth in a flood of words, mostly questions about the forthcoming duel.

Jess responded with noncommittal grunts up until Dudley asked him, "Who's gonna second for you?"

He raised a brow and peered at the shopkeeper in the dim glow of the overhead lamp.

"You wanna do it?" he asked.

Silence.

Sudden and heavy.

Dudley looked like a small bald owl with a mouse stuck crossways in its gullet. His Adam's apple worked up his throat, disappeared into the shadow under his chin, then dropped down, bounced on his collarbone, and rose again.

"Jesse, I . . . I'll tell you frankly — Hash Harker is about the best customer I got. He's the style-setter for this end of the county. Where he buys, that's where everybody buys. If he was to give up shopping here and take his custom to the county seat, half the rest of the folks around'd do the same."

"So you wouldn't want to chance losing his trade?" Jess said.

Dudley nodded faintly.

"What if he was to get killed in the duel?"

"That wouldn't matter so much. Not so long

118

as he didn't stop trading here first."

"What about us Wileys? We're good customers, too, ain't we?"

"I'd surely hate to lose the Wiley trade."

"What if you was to have to choose betwixt one or the other?"

"Jesse, I wish you wouldn't put it that way."

Jess studied Dudley thoughtfully, then said, "I don't reckon you'd make a hell of a good second nohow."

"No. No, I surely wouldn't," Dudley agreed.

"I want a new shirt," Jess said.

The stock was meager, but Dudley was anxious to please. He hauled out every shirt in the place — too big, too small, and in between. The one Jess picked was blue and white, with big bright checks. Dudley wrapped it for him. Carrying the parcel under his arm, he left for the barbershop.

The Gentlemen's Exclusive Tonsorial Parlor, Matt Matthews proprietor, was tucked in between the Boston Emporium and an abandoned building that had once been intended for a bank. The red and white ribbons that fluttered from the pole in front of the barbershop meant exactly what they advertised. The town physician was averse to surgery, so Matt Matthews continued in the ancient traditions of his trade, leeching, cutting, and pulling teeth as well as shaving, shearing, and providing bathing facilities.

Matthews was a portly but gainly man who hadn't needed his own services above the ears for a decade or more. In his spare time, he experimented extensively with store-bought and home-brewed hair restorers, none of which had worked, but at least one of which had imparted a permanent glossy brilliance to his scalp.

It was a truly beautiful scalp, as smooth as a China egg, and with a similar translucent glow. It was the exact shade of pink as the widow Grandly's best genuine silk lace-trimmed pantaloons, a secret Mrs. Grandly shared only with a pomade drummer named Feste out of St. Louis who made a point of stopping over at the Family Boardinghouse twice each year, and with Matt Matthews himself.

There were two customers ahead of Jess in the tonsorial parlor. Matthews had just finished wrapping a hot towel over the face of the one in the chair. The rest of the man was covered by a large striped cloth. Only a pair of trousered shins and button shoes showed. Jess didn't recognize them.

The other customer was the town physician, Ali Ibn, who sat waiting on the bench by the door. He was a small dark man with a few streaks of gray in his curly black hair. His teeth were very white, very even, the envy of all the women and most of the men around Hardly. He flashed them at Jess.

"Good morning, my friend," he said, making a gesture of invitation toward the space on the bench beside him.

Jess had a feeling Ali Ibn wanted to talk to

him. He supposed the man wanted to ask questions about the duel, the way Dudley had. He nodded in reply and looked toward the barber.

" 'Morning, Jesse," Matthews said. His glistening scalp flashed in a stray beam of sunlight as he bobbed his head in greeting.

" 'Morning. Looks like you're a mite busy."

"Not at all. I won't be long here, and the Doc only just wants a shave." Matthews looked appraisingly at Jess. "You'll want a shave and haircut both?"

"And a bath."

"For the partying tonight, eh?"

"Uh-huh."

"You just make yourself comfortable. Soon as I'm through here, I'll start the bath water to heat up." Matthews waved toward the bench.

Ali Ibn showed Jess his teeth again.

"I could come back later," Jess suggested, hoping he could somehow evade another questioning about the duel.

Matthews shook his head. It gleamed as if with an inner light of its own. "No, you'd better wait, else you'll find yourself at the far end of a long line. I expect I'll be having customers through here right regular all day today, getting slicked up for the festivities."

With a resigned sigh, Jess nodded agreement.

Ali Ibn gave him another display of teeth and made another small gesture of invitation.

Jess supposed he'd have to sit down and talk to the man eventually. But not yet. He set his par-

121

cel on the bench, then pulled off his hat and carefully racked it next to the suit coat and derby hanging on the peg tree. Scanning the shop, he hunted some way to stall.

Against the back wall, next to the entrance to the room that held the bathtub, there stood a tall mahogany cupboard with glass doors. On its shelves were displayed a large jar of leeches, an assortment of nickel-plated surgical and dental tools, and a pad of black velvet setting off a collection of pulled teeth of which Matthews was especially proud. Some, like the huge molar with the heavy hooked roots, were there because they represented particularly difficult cases that had tried his skill to its limits. Others, like the bicuspid in the middle, represented noted patients who had honored Matthews' shop. The bicuspid, which was without flaw, had come from the mouth of Big Jim Boohm himself. It hadn't needed pulling, but Matthews had wanted a souvenir of the occasion.

Jess fastened his gaze on the cabinet. Hooking his thumbs in his pockets, he ambled over and feigned interest in its contents.

"Did I ever tell you how I come to pull that there bicuspid?" Matthews began eagerly. "It belonged to Big Jim Boohm, the Builder. Happened one Sunday morning when —"

"Yeah," Jess interrupted. "You told me."

"Did I tell you, Doc?"

Ali Ibn nodded.

Matthews tried again. "That there big old molar, the one on the right in the second row front, that one come from —"

"Ezekiel W. Trot," Jess said. "It was the last tooth he had in his whole head, and it took you an hour and a half to make his jaw let loose of it."

Crushed, Matthews mumbled, "Uh-huh."

"Jesse, my friend," Ali Ibn called at Jess's back. "There is a matter I wish to discuss with you."

With a sigh, Jess turned away from the cabinet. Resigning himself to conversation, he settled next to the doctor.

Matt Matthews returned to the customer under the hot towel, which had cooled considerably by now.

Ali Ibn looked solemnly into Jess's face and said, "I have a problem."

"Huh?"

"It concerns my son, Hassan."

Jess looked blankly at him.

"You know Hassan?" the doctor continued, evidently misunderstanding Jess's expression. "The dark attractive youth who is so much in the company of your small sister, July."

The doctor spoke an oddly ornamented English with a faint accent. His introduction to the language of his adopted land had been from gamblers and graders when he was packing camels for a road crew. When he'd moved on into more polite society, he had embarked on a project of improving his manner of speaking. Studying under the Reverend P. Jonathan

Seven, he had overcompensated.

"You have seen Hassan more recently than I, I am certain," he said to Jess. "In truth, I rarely see the lad at all. I trust he is well?"

"Seen him yesterday with July. He looked fit."

"Yes, it would seem the two of them are always together." Ali Ibn sounded wistful. But not unhappy. "A most charming child, July. Intelligent, eager for knowledge, self-reliant. Excellent traits for a child in such rugged country as ours is."

"Unh," Jess answered, unsure of the doctor's meaning.

"In some ways she reminds me of my own delightful Dawn Woman. Of a more imposing will than Dawn Woman, perhaps, but that is well. It serves a man that he have a strong and useful woman to take to his bosom."

"Unh," Jess said again, for much the same reason.

"And the boy? My Hassan. What is your opinion of him?"

"I got nothing against him."

Ali Ibn seemed both disappointed and pleased. He said, "You think well of him, then?"

"Uh-huh."

"Your family also thinks well of him?"

"I reckon."

"They'd not oppose the match?"

It all came clear. Jess squinted at the doctor, then shrugged. "If it's what July wants, I reckon."

"Ah." Ali Ibn sounded quite pleased. Completely satisfied. "Well enough."

Matthews spoke up. "I'll be with you in a minute, Doc. And I'll get that bathing water heating up for you, Jesse."

He began to unwind the towel from the face of the man in the chair. As the customer's features were unveiled, Jess recognized them. They belonged to the derby-topped little man who had been on the coach yesterday. The one who'd taken a shot at him.

Matthews tilted up the headrest, and the customer in the barber chair opened his eyes. He saw a man of long bony features, hairy jaw, and prominent teeth, gazing curiously at him. He recognized the man.

This was the bandit who had stopped the stagecoach yesterday. The same one at whom he, Weston Finlay, had fired his new nickel-plated pocket pistol.

Weston Finlay was overwhelmed by a sudden vision of this highwayman wreaking vengeance upon his person here and now. With a sense of terrible tragedy, he saw his well-planned life ending abruptly, long before the conclusion he had intended for it.

He decided that if his time had come, he could face it as manfully as the traditions of the American West required. He tried to meet the highwayman's eyes. But his own eyes clamped shut and refused to open again.

He sat enclosed in darkness, awaiting his fate.

He sat for what seemed an hour — two hours — days — an eternity. He thought that his constitution, always considered most feeble, could stand it no longer. His body would fail in its vital functions. He would suffer the mortal embarrassment of dropping dead where he sat before the brigand's bullet ever reached him.

He could stand this waiting no longer. His eyes flashed open. He stared at the man seated in front of him.

" 'Morning," Jess said, touching his fingers to the place where his hat brim would have been if he'd had on his hat. He hoped the little man had calmed down since yesterday. He was in no mood for being shot at right now.

Weston Finlay suddenly felt unreal. None of it seemed real. Not the barber, or the man with the bright white teeth, or the highwayman, or himself. He was in the middle of a nightmare.

Without will or choice, he blinked, bolted from the barber chair, and lunged through the open door.

As Weston Finlay shot out of the barbershop, Matt Matthews frowned in puzzlement. He exchanged curious glances with Ali Ibn. They both looked at Jess.

"He kinda left in a hurry, didn't he?" Jess mumbled.

Ali Ibn nodded and said, "A stranger to Hardly, I believe."

"He come in on the coach yesterday," Matthews told them. "I hear tell he's going right back out on it when it leaves again."

"That so?" Jess said.

"He seemed to be rather an excitable sort," Ali Ibn commented.

Jess suggested, "Maybe he kinda recollected something all of a sudden."

"Kinda forgot something all of a sudden, too," Matthews said, hooking a thumb toward the hat and coat on the peg tree. He plucked the derby off the tree and set it on his head. It perched precariously high above his ears.

"Don't fit," Jess told him.

Ali Ibn said, "I would imagine he will return for them."

"Hope so," Matthews muttered as he replaced the hat on its peg. "He didn't pay me, either."

He started into the back room to fire up the boiler that would heat the bath water. Pausing at the curtained doorway, he looked back at Jess. "I been hearing about this duel you and Hash Harker are gonna have."

"Uh-huh."

"Who's gonna be second for you?"

"Ain't got nobody yet," Jess said. "Maybe . . . ?"

Matthews disappeared behind the curtain.

Jess turned to Ali Ibn. "Doc, I wonder if maybe you'd stand second for me?"

Ali Ibn hesitated a long thoughtful moment, then said, "My friend, would you agree that in this fair state of Texas, this fair town of Hardly,

127

the office of physician and pharmacist is an office of trust?"

"I reckon."

"Alas, it is written: 'Any citizen of this state who shall fight a duel with deadly weapons, or who shall act as second, or knowingly aid and assist, in any manner, those thus offending, shall be deprived of holding any office of trust or profit under this state.' "

Apologetically, Jess said, "I'm sorry, Doc. If I'd knowed it was against your religion, I wouldn't even of asked."

Matt Matthews returned from the back room. He picked up a razor, flipped it open, and brandished it toward the barber chair. "Ready, Doc?"

Ali Ibn gave Jess a small regretful smile. Settling himself in the chair, he closed his eyes.

"What about you, Matt?" Jess asked.

Matthews reached for a strop. Holding it out, he began to stroke the razor vigorously up and down it.

"Me?" he said. "Second in a duel?"

"Uh-huh."

"Unh-ugh."

"Why not?"

"You see, Jesse, it's this way." He paused to test the blade, then started in stropping it again. "I got a problem."

"Huh?"

He set down the razor and held up his hands. They were pudgy and pink, fringed on the backs

128

with fine pale fuzz. Turning them, he gazed at them as if they held something very precious.

"You know I'm a musical artist. My barbering and surgering and tooth-pulling — them's my livelihood. But my fiddling, that's my *life*. It's my hands, Jesse. I seen men as lost a joint or a whole finger or even a hand right up to the elbow by having some kind of a pistol-gun go off all un-expected on them. Maybe just plain blowing up — *boom!*" He made a wide flinging gesture with both hands.

"If a man's a second in a duel," he continued, "he's got to load up a pistol. I couldn't do that. I don't intend not never to touch no guns of no kind. I got to look out for my hands."

He turned them over again, admiring them.

"Oh," Jess said.

Eyes still closed, Ali Ibn gave a nod of sympa-thy.

Matthews returned his hands to their job of barbering. He took a mug down from the rack, moistened the brush, and began to work up a lather.

Jess leaned back to wait.

CHAPTER 12

Junie Wiley was troubled in her mind. She was concerned about the impending duel. The thought of either Hash or Jess getting hurt, maybe killed, appalled her.

She had hoped that, as Hash's second, Dominic would be able to protect both principals somehow. She had less faith in Jacob. His intentions might always be good, but she had to admit that sometimes his judgment wasn't.

She'd slept troubled, risen early, and sat worrying through three cups of well-spiced tea. She hadn't come up with any solution to her problem, but she had decided on a way to soothe her nerves and take her mind off her worries for a while. She was going to buy herself a new bonnet.

As Junie made her way toward the Gen. Mdse., a buggy was making its way toward town in a huff of dust. The gray between the shafts was Hash Harker's Messenger-bred trotter, the one he never let anyone else drive. But the man at the reins this morning was Jacob Wiley. Miss Lucinda Cummins of Fairwater, Virginia, was at his side.

Jacob Wiley was troubled in his mind. Last

night he had been formally introduced to one of Hash Harker's house guests. The other one, a Mrs. Delphinia Quick (widowed), had been abed, indisposed, when Jacob arrived at the Harker house. But Miss Lucinda was still up and about.

And when Hash presented her to Jacob, she'd smiled. Jacob hadn't felt the same since.

When he'd failed to win his bet with Dominic yesterday, he'd felt a mild ache in his pride. When Miss Lucinda smiled at him, he'd suddenly felt a lot worse. He'd had his chance to kiss those pretty pink lips and he'd missed it. Smiling back at her, he promised himself that if he ever got the chance again, he sure wouldn't let it get by him.

But what chance would he have? Here was Miss Lucinda, soon to marry up with Hash Harker, and here was he, Jacob, promised to second in a duel on behalf of Miss Lucinda's honor against his own brother on account of his brother had taken the advantage he'd missed. He had a notion it wouldn't be at all proper for him, as Harker's second, to up and do the same thing his brother had done. Leastways not until after the duel was over.

To Jacob's disappointment, Miss Lucinda had just barely said hello, and then she'd off and disappeared. But Hash had broken out the brandy then, which was some consolation. The two of them had sat up drinking and discussing the duel until the small hours of the morning. It had all sounded very complicated to Jacob. He'd had

131

trouble keeping his mind on it.

He'd slept sound, as usual, dreaming of Miss Lucinda and of buzzards. He disregarded the buzzards. Those were common enough in his dreams. But the images of Miss Lucinda lingered after he'd wakened. He was resting up from a hearty breakfast, thoughtfully recollecting the dreams in detail, when he saw her in the flesh again.

Miss Lucinda Cummins was troubled in her mind. She had journeyed from her home to this distant land to marry a man she'd never met. Her parents, who were of excellent stock, but who had been in financial straits ever since some difficulty concerning the Credit Mobilier, had arranged the match. They had assured her that love would quickly follow the marriage. As a dutiful daughter, and because she'd read such wonderful things about the men of the American West, she had willingly accepted their decision. Now, though, she was afraid all was not proceeding according to plan.

She found Hash Harker personable and rather attractive, and she supposed she might in time have learned to really care for him in a proper wifely manner, if it hadn't been for one thing.

Jess Wiley.

In all her young life, Miss Lucinda had never been kissed before except on the cheek or, playfully, on the tip of the nose by close relatives. No lips had ever touched hers before, even in early childhood.

Then, quite suddenly, her world had exploded.

Reading the wonderful dime novels that her parents had so absolutely forbidden, she'd learned myriad words about soulmates, ethereal passion, and true love. Now, though, all those extravagances of language seemed pitifully inadequate to her own situation. She felt herself in the grip of most unique emotions. She felt herself possessed by a love more intense, more pure, more true, than ever a mortal woman had known before.

She was certain that, without Jess Wiley, she would pine away, a pallid tragic figure beyond all hope of succor.

Jacob Wiley came as a shock to her. He looked very much like his brother. He had the same knobby lankiness she'd found so charming in Jess, and the same kind of opaquely dark eyes that she felt were unfathomable in their depths, and the same sort of thin mobile lips spreading away from teeth like the mellowed ivory keys of a harpsichord. How she loved the harpsichord!

Fascinated and fearful, Miss Lucinda had struggled to contain a turmoil of emotion as she was introduced to Jacob Wiley. She'd smiled politely, managed a spoken hello, and then had fled to her bedroom to ponder her befuddlement.

She'd slept fitfully, dreaming things she would never have admitted. She woke knowing she'd dreamed, but unable to recall a single image.

When she learned that Harker was away from

the house on business, and her chaperon still indisposed, she discovered there was some shopping she absolutely *had* to do before the party
tonight. Since she could hardly drive herself into
town, she had no alternative but to ask Jacob.

Delighted, Jacob had helped himself to the
buggy and the gray trotter that was Harker's
pride and joy. When he'd given her a hand into
the buggy, Miss Lucinda had smiled at him and
thanked him. He'd settled in the driver's seat
next to her, anticipating a very pleasant outing.

But beyond the simple thank-you, Miss
Lucinda found herself at a loss for words. She sat
in the seat at Jacob's side as stiff as a cemetery
sculpture, and just as silent.

Jacob tried talking about the weather. When
he said how hot it was, she nodded. When he
said how much they needed rain, she nodded
again. When he said what a fine horse the gray
was, she nodded to that, too. When he asked her
was she looking forward to the partying tonight,
she just gave him another quick tight-lipped
nod.

Discouraged, he sank into a pouting silence of
his own. As he slipped deeper and deeper into
brooding thoughts, he slapped the gray into a
faster and faster trot. Finally the despairing
horse broke into a gallop. The buggy bounced
and jounced wildly over the wheel-rutted road.
Miss Lucinda clung to the grab iron with both
small white-gloved hands, fearful that she was
about to fall out, or be deathly ill, or perhaps both.

134

Jacob reached a sudden decision. He hauled back sharply on the reins. The gray tossed up its head, snorting, as it tried to stop. The weight of the buggy rammed against the breeching. The horse staggered. The buggy lurched, and Miss Lucinda was certain that it was going to topple over. But then the horse was standing steady, and the buggy rested shivering on its springs, still upright.

Very slowly and deliberately, Jacob set down the reins. He turned to face Miss Lucinda. His hands reached toward her.

She stared at him in total bewilderment.

He grasped her shoulders. With no preliminaries, he planted his mouth on hers.

Her lips parted to him.

The rest of her, astonished, sat stock still.

When the kiss had been completed, Jacob lifted the reins and urged the gray into a trot again. He sat grinning to himself, no longer concerned over Miss Lucinda's silence.

Miss Lucinda barely noticed that the buggy was in motion once more. Through her confusion, she saw only one thing clearly. She had made a most startling discovery. Contrary to the teachings of her parents and the small forbidden books, she knew now that it was quite possible for a woman to be — absolutely and beyond salvation — in love with two men at once.

Within the dimness of the Gen. Mdse., McDonald Dudley lifted his hand lantern and

135

aimed its feeble glow at Junie Wiley's face. She had a mirror in her hand. A straw bonnet spangled with pink primroses fashioned of dyed feathers perched on her head. Pursing her lips, she studied her reflection in the mirror.

Dudley watched her intently, trying to decide whether she liked the bonnet enough to pay him the asking price for it. He could knock it down a bit. He'd have been willing to sell it at cost just to recover his investment. But he'd rather not.

Junie pouted as she considered. She wondered how much she could bargain Dudley down on the price. She was about to make a disparaging comment for openers when she heard the rattle of a buggy stopping just outside. It sounded like Hash Harker's rig. She smiled as she turned toward the door.

But the man who appeared silhouetted in the doorway wasn't Hash. It looked like Jacob. And there was a woman at his side.

Jacob hesitated. He knew how his sister felt about Hash Harker. He wasn't too certain how she'd feel about the woman Harker planned to marry. He didn't think he ought to let the two of them meet right now. Not while he was around to get caught in the middle. But before he could shove Miss Lucinda back outside, or turn and run himself, Junie was calling him by name.

" 'Morning, Junie," he mumbled at her.

She put down the mirror and hurried toward him. She stopped in front of him, but she looked at Miss Lucinda. It was the quick, deep, appraising kind of look a woman gives only to another woman of her own age.

Miss Lucinda returned it in kind, and more so.

The girl that Miss Lucinda saw before her lacked style and was far from fashionable, but the simple sun-touched face was pretty, and the body under the common calico frock showed more than a suggestion of well-filled curves. Whoever she was, this country girl was admittedly attractive. And worst of all, she knew Jacob well enough to call him Jacob.

Jacob wanted a drink. He couldn't remember ever wanting a drink as much as he did now.

"Junie," he said hoarsely. "This here is Miss Lucinda Virginia of Fairwater, Cummins."

Junie didn't need to be told. From the first long look, she'd known without a doubt that this was the girl who'd come here to marry Hash Harker.

She said, "Miss Lucinda, you don't know how much I've been looking forward to meeting you."

The smallest and politest of all possible small polite smiles struggled into existence on Miss Lucinda's mouth.

Then Jacob remembered to say, "Miss Lucinda, this here is my sister Junie."

Sister!

Relief washed through Miss Lucinda. A sister was no competition. This wasn't someone who might steal Jess's or Jacob's love, but rather was a woman of her own age whom she might take for a friend. One in whom she might confide. One who could tell her more about the two men she loved, and whose companionship could bring her closer to both of them.

She held out her arms to Junie as if she were greeting a sister of her own, one dearly beloved and long lost.

Junie's smile widened as she opened her arms to this woman who was to be Hash Harker's bride. From the time Hash first told her he was bringing in a girl to marry, Junie had been given to concerned speculation. In fact, it was because of the forthcoming marriage that she'd failed to take her French medicine.

It wasn't that she expected the marriage to make much difference between her and Hash. After all, he'd sent for this woman to be an ornament he could take with him to the county seat and the state capital. She was meant to oversee the keeping of his house and to tend to all those little wifely duties that Junie would have liked for her own. But the bride-to-be wasn't someone Hash had fallen in love with. She wasn't likely to interfere much with an already existing warm and firm friendship.

Nevertheless, Junie had decided a child could give added strength to the relationship. Even if Hash should happen to get to liking his wife, he would still want to visit with his child and its mother, wouldn't he?

So Junie had skipped her French medicine. And she had speculated on whether the mail-order bride would be someone she could be friends with and learn about city fashions from.

Miss Lucinda was slender and wan, soft-cheeked and well-gussied, just like the tinted copperplate engravings from *Harper's* and *Godey's*. And with her arms outheld, she seemed even more friendly than Junie had dared hope.

As if in confirmation, Miss Lucinda said with almost breathless eagerness, "We must be friends! The very best of friends!"

"We must!" Junie echoed.

Jacob sighed, and wished he had a drink.

The girls broke their embrace and stepped back to look each other over again, this time with approval.

With an attempt to sound sincere, Miss Lucinda said, "What an absolutely beautiful bonnet!"

"Do you like it?" Junie said. She'd always felt she had natural good taste. She was pleased to have her opinion endorsed by someone of experience. She was positive now that she and Miss Lucinda would be the best of friends.

"It's absolutely adorable," Miss Lucinda said hurriedly. She was eager to get past the preliminaries and start making woman-talk with the sister of the two men she loved.

Junie was just as eager. She turned to her brother. "Jacob, you ain't no use to us now. Why don't you go off and get a drink and talk to Dominic awhile or something while Miss Lucinda and me get acquainted?"

"Please call me 'Cindy,' " Miss Lucinda said.

Jacob grinned at his sister, touched his hat brim to Miss Lucinda, wheeled, and strode off toward the Grand Palace of the Golden Dragon.

Junie shot a sharp look at McDonald Dudley. He had his back to them and was tinkering with boxes on a shelf while he eavesdropped.

She said, "I don't think I want the bonnet after all."

He swung around to face her. "But — but after what this nice lady said . . ."

"It's far too expensive."

"I — uh — er —"

"Now, if it was a dollar or so less . . ."

"A dollar!" Dudley looked aghast.

Junie nodded solemnly.

"Maybe fifty cents," he mumbled, sounding most reluctant.

"Six bits?" she suggested.

He nodded.

"Put it on my chit," she told him. Then she turned to Miss Lucinda. "Let's us stroll around a bit and talk."

They left the store arm in arm.

CHAPTER 13

Jody had arrived in Hardly at a hungry gallop. He dropped reins over the hitch rail in front of Mrs. Grandly's Family Boardinghouse and rushed inside, eager for a decent meal. When he'd finished stuffing himself at Mrs. Grandly's table, he strolled over to the Grand Palace of the Golden Dragon for an after-breakfast drink or two.

The door of the Palace was wide open, and Ezekiel W. Trot and the Reverend P. Jonathan Seven were inside at their usual table, continuing their discussion over corn whiskey and a bottle of rather potent but socially acceptable sherry respectively. Neither paid him any mind as he ambled in.

Dominic was behind the bar, busy as usual running his dirty barcloth over dirty glasses. Jody gave him a nod and a mumble. Dominic set up a shot of corn whiskey.

"How you been?" Dom asked.

Jody answered with a dull grunt, poured down the shot, and shoved the glass toward Dom for a refill.

Dom filled it again and said sociably, "How's the duel coming?"

Jody grunted again and finished off the second

shot. He hoped he'd made it clear he didn't feel like conversation. The meal had settled his stomach, but right now he was real unsettled in his mind.

Ever since he'd turned old enough to be allowed into the saloon, Jody'd had a problem. The girls who lived upstairs always ragged him about his being young. They refused to take him seriously about anything. The older he got, the worse this bothered him.

Now he was man enough to put down several corn whiskeys without choking on them, and he had a gun of his own, and he felt more than ready for the girls to treat him like a full-grown man, but they still acted like he was just a little boy.

How the hell would they *ever* come to take him seriously if word got around that his Pa was a buzzard?

He finished off a third shot and started out back toward the privy. Just as he walked up to the door with the little quarter-moon cut into it, it opened. Nancy stepped out.

Nancy was hardly any older than Jody, but she'd been Jess's regular girl for a while now, and she'd always acted like that put her on a lot higher horse than Jody could ever hope to be on. That really chafed at him, even worse than when the other girls ragged him. He felt downright resentful toward her as he dutifully touched his hat brim and said good morning to her.

She surprised him by giving him a real friendly smile. She astonished him by stopping him on the path and asking him to come up to her room and talk to her awhile.

Fearful that she meant to play some kind of trick on him, he tried to say no. But it came out yes.

She gave him another smile then, and went on her way, leaving him feeling oddly excited and awfully apprehensive.

He hurried through his business in the privy as fast as he could, and he was still buttoning his breeches as he left. He slammed the saloon door behind him and dashed up the stairs.

When he knocked at Nancy's door, it opened to him, and she smiled at him again.

Bewildered and befuddled, he followed her gesture into the room. It was a very small room, with a cot, a tall skinny wardrobe, and a little bedside table with a lamp all jammed into it. There was hardly enough standing space left for two people to move comfortably in.

Nancy motioned for him to close the door. When he did it, the room seemed to get even smaller. He wasn't actually touching her, but he could feel her nearness, and his skin got all crawly. He felt real warm. A little bit like he was suffocating.

"How you been, Jody?" she said.

He tried to answer, but all he managed was a funny noise in his throat.

"Like a drink?" she asked.

He made the same noise again.

She took it for acceptance and bent over to

pull something from under the bed. As she bent, her hip brushed his thigh. The touch sent shivers all through him. He had a sudden thought of grabbing her and flinging her down on her back. The idea fascinated and horrified him.

She pulled a little traveling case from under the cot and took out a couple of drinking glasses. When she held them out toward Jody, he couldn't think what to do about it. She had to put them into his hands. Then she took her own personal bottle of good Kentucky bourbon from the case and filled the two glasses. The liquor sloshed around in them, and Jody realized his hands were trembling. He didn't want her to see that. He wanted to put the glasses down, but there was nowhere to put them except on the bedside table, and Nancy was between him and it, and he couldn't reach it without shoving past her, and there wasn't room enough, and it sure seemed awful hot and stuffy, and he sure wished his hands would stop shaking like that.

Nancy set the bottle on the table and took one of the glasses from him. She lifted it toward him in the gesture of a toast, then sipped from it. He immediately emptied the other glass down his gullet. The bourbon was as smooth and silky as pure branch water, but he almost choked on it. Sputtering, he managed to get it down.

Nancy didn't mock him. She just picked up the bottle and refilled the glass. Then she sat down on the bed and patted the space at her side.

He realized that she meant for him to sit next to her. He recalled his thought of flinging her down on her back, and it seemed to him that he wouldn't have to do anything like that. She was leading the way.

A wild elation filled him. He gulped down the fresh drink with no trouble at all, then flopped onto the cot at her side.

And just as he started a hand toward her, she ruined it all.

She asked, "What's wrong with Jesse these days? He just ain't the way he used to be at all."

The elation drained right out of Jody. He'd never before felt so empty in all his life. He told himself he should have known she wouldn't want anything from *him,* except it had to do with his brother. He had half a mind to get up and stalk out and not talk to her at all. But she was so close to him that he could smell the scent of her, and her voice flowed into his head sweet as honey.

"Jesse ain't no fun no more," she was saying. "He's just getting to be a grumpy old toadfrog. He don't hardly pay me no proper attention at all."

"You're going to the partying tonight with him, ain't you?" Jody muttered, sniffing at her aroma.

She shrugged. "I don't know. I'd sure like to know what's got into him."

"I reckon it's this duel thing," Jody heard himself say. Without exactly meaning to, he found he was telling her all about it and how Jess had got into trouble by kissing Hash Harker's girl friend, and even how he, himself, had up and shot Whisk Shaker.

Then, to his astonishment, he discovered that he was telling her how his own mother had said his Pa was dead and had come back as a buzzard. Even as he spoke, he expected her to burst out laughing.

But she didn't do that at all.

She put a hand on his shoulder. A very warm, sympathetic hand. And the next thing he knew, she was sitting right there on the bed beside him with her thigh nestled against his, and it was *him*, not Jess, they were talking about.

Jacob was smiling smugly to himself when he ambled into the Grand Palace of the Golden Dragon. As he settled into his usual spot at the bar, Dominic nodded to him, set a shot glass in front of him, and filled it.

"To wimmin!" Jacob said. He gulped the glass empty and set it down for a refill.

Behind him, in the corner by the window, Ezekiel W. Trot and the Reverend P. Jonathan Seven bent their heads together and spoke intently to each other. Neither had paid any attention when Jacob came in. Neither looked up when Jess strode through the door.

Turning, Jacob saw his brother all shaved, shorn, scrubbed, and bedecked in a new shirt.

He grinned and said, "My, ain't you purty this morning."

"Unh," Jess replied, setting his elbows on the bar.

Dominic put a glass in front of him and filled it. "How's the duel coming?"

"I ain't got no second yet." Jess paused to down the drink. "How about you, Dom? You know what these things is all about. Will you second for me?"

"Hell no!"

"Why not?"

"I ain't having nothing more to do with that damn duel, except maybe to watch it happen." As he spoke, Dominic set out a third glass. He filled it carelessly, spilling some over the side. He didn't bother to wipe it up. Leaning his own elbows on the bar, he sighed morosely and said, "That duel ain't made me nothing but sorrow."

"You?" Jess said in surprise.

Jacob asked curiously, "How come?"

"With Junie. We had us one hell of a set-to last night."

"Huh? Over the duel?" Jess said.

"Uh-huh. About me quitting as Harker's second."

"She was mad over that?"

"Uh-huh."

"How come?" Jacob said. "I'll take care of being Hash's second. Didn't you tell her that?"

"Uh-huh. I dunno. Sometimes she ain't a easy

147

woman to figure out. Sometimes I wish I hadn't met up with her."

Jess asked, "How come?"

"Oh, I dunno." Dominic emptied his glass, then poked a finger into the spilled whiskey on the bar. He drew it out into a wet line. "I dunno. I got a notion if it wasn't for Junie, I could up and find me a woman that would marry me with a preacher and all that. Take my name and raise me some young'uns as would call me Pa."

Jacob snorffled through his nose. He couldn't see why Dominic got so het up over something as unimportant as a marrying ceremony.

Jess said, "If that's what you really want, why don't you go ahead after it? Why do you stick with Junie when you know she ain't gonna change her mind?"

"I dunno."

"Pomegranate," Ezekiel W. Trot said loudly.

"Apple," the Reverend P. Jonathan Seven answered him.

Dominic stared at the wet spot on the bar. Without moving his head, he lifted a brow and slanted an eye at Jess. "I reckon it's just uncommon easy for a man to stay where he is, and uncommon hard for him to pick up and move."

"Hell, I do what I damn please," Jacob said with a grin.

But Jess nodded in sympathy. He had his own longings to pick up and move, and he hadn't done it. Seemed as how he kept going on the way he was going just because it was the way he was going.

Dominic was right, he thought.

Jacob's glass was full again, and his thoughts were on Miss Lucinda. He lifted the glass and said, "To wimmin!"

"Unh," Jess said, remembering Nance. She ought to be awake and around by now. He downed his drink and headed for the stairs.

Jacob gave Dominic a knowing wink. Dominic answered with a mournful sigh.

Upstairs, Jess rapped at the door to Nance's room.

Her voice came clearly through the panels. "Who is it?"

"Me," he said.

"Jesse?"

"Yeah."

"Oh."

There was a moment of silence. Then she called, "Just a minute."

After another moment, he heard a creaking of floorboards and the scrape of the latch bolt. The door edged open far enough for one eyeball to peek out.

"What is it?" she asked with a noticeable lack of enthusiasm.

"You still figure on going to the partying to-night?"

"Uh-huh."

"You still figure on me taking you?"

She hesitated. Slowly she said, "Jesse, I . . . I kind . . . well, I . . ."

"You *ain't* figuring on me taking you?"

"Things ain't the same as they used to be with us, are they, Jesse?"

He thought about it a moment. "No, I reckon they ain't."

"We ought to own up to it, shouldn't we?"

He nodded.

"You mind?" she asked.

He shook his head.

She smiled at him. "You're really kinda sweet."

He grinned back at her, feeling downright relieved. "Reckon I'll see you there, then?"

"Uh-huh."

Touching his fingers to his hat brim, he backed off and headed downstairs again.

In their corner, Ezekiel W. Trot and the Reverend P. Jonathan Seven were still exchanging words.

"Pomegranate."

"Apple."

At the bar, Jacob was standing with both hands empty. He was using them to draw curving lines in the air as he described Miss Lucinda Cummins of Fairwater, Virginia.

Dominic leaned his elbows on the bar and cupped his chin in his hands, his thoughts elsewhere.

Jess stepped up to the bar and grunted. Dominic recognized the order. He interrupted his wandering thoughts long enough to refill the glass he'd left waiting for Jess.

Jacob turned to his brother. "You really got to meet her, Jesse. She's sure something else!"

"What?"

"Miss Lucinda. I been getting to know her. You really got to meet her."

Jess felt he'd met Miss Lucinda well enough in the Gen. Mdse. He recollected her arms around his neck. It seemed they'd been tightening on him like a noose. He mumbled, "I've met her all I want to."

Jacob frowned. "What you mean by that?"

His tone spoke to Jess more than his words. With a touch of apprehension, Jess said, "What you carrying on about?"

"That Miss Lucinda." Jacob's frown turned into a grin that answered Jess's question completely.

"You've went and got all calf-eyed over her, ain't you?"

Jacob just kept grinning.

Things were getting downright confusing, Jess thought. Here it was, Junie wanted Hash Harker, and Harker wanted Miss Lucinda, and Miss Lucinda wanted Jess, and Jacob wanted Miss Lucinda, and on top of all that, Harker wanted Jess's blood. And there was no telling what that damn buzzard that went around claiming to be Deke Wiley wanted.

He said, "I think I got to get."

"What you gonna do about a second for the duel?" Dominic asked him before he could turn away.

"Find me one, I reckon."

"Who?"

He shrugged.

"Listen here, Dom," Jacob said. "I tell you, ain't nobody around these parts never seen nothing like this Miss Lucinda before. She's pure thoroughbred from head to hock."

"You seen her hocks?" Dominic asked curiously.

"Apple," said the Reverend P. Jonathan Seven.

Ezekiel W. Trot replied, "Pomegranate."

Jess stepped up to the batwings and paused. He'd caught the sound of a woman's voice just outside. A very lilting, very Eastern voice, distorted now with a pang of distress. "But I can't possibly go in *there*. It just isn't *proper*. A *lady* would never be seen in such a place."

The voice that answered belonged to his sister Junie. "Why not? Hell, Cindy, ain't nobody in there but just plain folk like my man, Dom, and likely Ezekiel W. Trot and the Reverend Seven. Looky, if a church feller like the Reverend can set in there all day glumping sherry, there can't be nothing wrong with the place, can there? I want you to meet Dom. And I got to pick up some brandy to flavor the tea."

"But —"

"We'll only just step inside and say hello and fetch the bottle. Then we'll head right on over to the house and have us some tea and talk."

"I . . . I —"

Jess could hear a wavering in Miss Lucinda's voice, as if she might actually give in to his sister. If she were coming in, he thought, he was going out. He leaned forward slightly to look over the batwings at the women.

At that instant, Miss Lucinda looked up. Her eyes met his.

"Jesse!" she shrieked. The word bespoke ponderous depths of pent emotion.

Jess turned and ran.

As he slammed out through the back door, he could hear the batwings squealing. He didn't look back. Outside, he wheeled around the corner of the building and dashed for the street. His horse was tied in front of the saloon. He was certain that, once in the saddle, he could escape.

CHAPTER 14

Miss Lucinda erupted through the batwings into the Grand Palace of the Golden Dragon without so much as an instant of thought about propriety, or anything else for that matter, except Jess Wiley. She'd seen him, and she wanted him, and she was midway past the bar, racing toward that back door he'd escaped through, when she realized that someone was calling her name.

The voice was a man's. A familiar voice. One that, in a brief time, she had come to cherish as if it were graven on her heart.

The voice of Jacob Wiley.

Stopping short, she spun to face him.

"Miss Lucinda," he said, beaming at her.

"Ma'am," Dominic said. He bobbed his head in a nod of greeting.

Miss Lucinda clutched at her skirts as she grabbed for her composure. Her face was suddenly burning all the way down to her knees. She felt as if she might melt into a puddle of appalled mush.

Then Junie was at her side, saying with a most wonderfully soothing aplomb, "Cindy, honey, this here cussed old coot is Dominic Johanssen. He's my man at the moment."

Miss Lucinda stumbled through what felt like the most inept curtsy she'd executed since, at the age of nine, she had first been required to practice her dancing lessons with a real live boy of the opposite — dare she think it? — sex.

"Dom," Junie continued. "You fetch out a bottle of that there good brandy for me and Cindy, huh?"

"Let me buy," Jacob said gallantly.

"We was gonna take the bottle over to the house," Junie told him.

He looked aghast. "Aw, come on, sis. Lemme set one up, huh? Just to be sociable."

Junie gave him a quick wink. To Miss Lucinda, she said, "What about it? Just one with the boys here 'fore we go on home?"

Miss Lucinda had no idea how to reply. She had never tasted anything stronger than home-made elderberry wine, and she had vowed that she'd never so much as touch fingertips with any man who indulged in strong spirits. But here she was, actually within a den of iniquity, and here was one of the only two men she would ever truly love, and he was offering her strong drink, and . . . and . . .

And it was indeed true that love conquered all, she thought wistfully as she nodded agreement.

Dom filled the glasses.

Cautiously she accepted one. She raised it, sniffing its aroma and wondering what it would do to her. She had been told that such stuff would destroy a woman's most precious virtue.

But love conquers all, she told herself. Including virtue.

Leaning her head back, she emptied the glass into her mouth. Sudden fire flowed down her throat. It kicked her in the stomach. Sputtering, choking, she dropped the glass and doubled over.

A heavy fist began pounding her between the shoulderblades. Jacob crooned at her, "Steady, there, steady."

Fingers caught her hand and shoved another glass into it. Junie said solicitously, "Drink this, honey."

Miss Lucinda was certain she'd never be able to drink anything again, ever. She shook her head and gasped for breath.

"It's sarsaparilla," Junie said. "Smooth as soothing syrup."

With effort Miss Lucinda got her head up and tipped the glass to her lips. Sweet cool liquid filled her mouth and streamed down her scorched throat. It eased the choking burning. She managed to get a good gulp of air into her lungs.

"Maybe you shouldn't take it straight right off," Junie said. She turned to Jacob. "I shoulda took her home and give it to her in tea."

Miss Lucinda slowly smiled. A rather pleasant warmth was spreading through her body. Her smile broadened. Cautiously, stammering, she suggested, "I . . . I might try again."

"Sure enough, ma'am." Dominic set up a new

glass for her. "It's on the house."

"Water that down some," Junie told him.

"With what?"

"Water."

"Oh."

He looked around uncertainly, then remembered the bucket he kept for washing glasses. He'd filled it fresh this morning and hardly used it yet. He ladled water from it into the brandy he'd just poured.

Taking the drink, Junie held it out to Miss Lucinda. "Here, honey, you drink it a little slower this time. You'll get the hang of it."

Grinning crookedly, but gamely, Miss Lucinda accepted. This time she emptied only half the glass into her mouth. It still burned painfully, but she was able to bear it. And the feeling it gave her was so nice. . . .

She cocked her head and eyed Jacob, admiring the harsh planes of his face, the hairy thickets of his brows, the rugged roughness of his unshaven jaw, the weather-chapped charm of his mouth. His teeth spread out before her, and she thought again of the keys of a harpsichord. She wished she had her harpsichord here. She'd play for them all. Especially for Jacob.

The warmth seemed to enfold her. She felt as if she were glowing, as if all the room were brightened by her own radiance. Yes, she advised herself, this was, indeed, the most beautiful world in the world.

Daintily she set her glass on the bar. She

turned her smile toward Jacob and asked, "May I have just a taste more?"

He grinned back at her. "You can have all you want, honey."

Junie poked him in the ribs. In answer to his querulous glance, she whispered, "It ain't no how proper to call another man's fiancy 'honey' right out in public, you big jackass."

"Why not?"

"It just ain't proper."

Jacob found he didn't much care. He shrugged and grinned again.

And Dominic set them up again, all around.

July and Hassan arrived in town soon after Jody. Turning on Main Street, they passed Mrs. Grandly's Family Boardinghouse. They took note of Jody's horse at the hitch rail.

Riding on past the Grand Palace of the Golden Dragon, they saw Jess's roan tied in front of the saloon. July assumed her brother was safe inside the Palace and since he couldn't have gotten to town much ahead of her, he'd likely be in the saloon for a while more. She figured she and Hassan had plenty of time to get a quick meal from Hassan's mother and be back at their spying before Jess came out and went elsewhere.

They left the pony tied behind the two-story adobe building where Ali Ibn maintained his pharmacy and his family home. Upstairs, in the living quarters, they ate beside a front window so that July could keep an eye on the saloon.

They'd both finished off first helpings and were well into seconds when July saw her sister Junie and Miss Lucinda Cummins stroll up to the door of the saloon and stop there.

"I think there's going to be some excitement now," July told Hassan.

He nodded in agreement.

Together they headed downstairs.

They were standing at the corner of the pharmacy, peering around it at the Palace, when Jess came racing around the saloon. As Jess flung himself into the roan's saddle, July was grabbing the reins of the pinto. By the time Jess reached the corner of Main and Sixth streets, July and Hassan were mounted and following at a discreet distance.

Jess had reached the edge of town at a gallop when he looked back to see if he were being followed. He was, all right. By July and Hassan. And by that buzzard, as well. He saw it making a low, lazy sweep over the town.

Could it really be Deke Wiley, he wondered.

He remembered suddenly that he still had business in Hardly. He still had to find himself a second for the duel. Hauling the roan down to a walk, he glanced around thoughtfully. Who else was left to ask?

"Jesse Wiley! Hold on there!" The voice was Whisk Shaker's.

Jess saw Whisk coming toward him from the

shade of the sycamore in the yard of the coach-line stable. A checkerboard with a game in progress sat on an upended keg under the tree, awaiting Deke Wiley's next move.

One of Whisk's sleeves was rolled up, showing a tattered dirt-colored rag that had been a bright white bandage the day before. A loop of faded gingham meant for a sling hung from his neck. The injured arm was at his side. He raised it to wave at Jess.

"I got to talk to you," he called.

Jess grunted in response.

"I got a problem," Whisk said.

Jess considered lighting out. He figured he'd heard more than enough problems these past few days. But it was true his brother had shot Whisk, and that sort of gave him a family obligation to be decently polite to the old man, least-ways till the wound had healed.

With worn patience, he swung one leg over the horse's withers and hooked his knee around the saddle horn. He rested an elbow on the knee and looked down at Whisk.

Whisk worked his jaw, spat into the dust, then stepped up and laid a hand on the roan's neck. He looked up at Jess.

"I got this here problem. I mean, Jesse, you ain't heard nothing from your Pa yet?"

"That's kinda hard to say."

"How come? Either you heard or you ain't."

"Either it's my Pa or it ain't."

"How's that again?"

"Ne'mind. Just say I ain't heard. What's your problem?"

"I'm gonna have to take the coach out again day after tomorrow. Got to keep her somewheres near to the schedule. Should take her out tomorrow. Put it off one more day. Can't put it off no longer than that. You understand?"

Jess nodded, wondering what the hell the old man was getting at.

"Thing is, is your Pa gonna be back before then or ain't he?"

Jess shrugged.

"If he ain't . . . Damn her all to swithers, Jesse, I got to make my move!"

"Move? Oh, your checker move, you mean?"

"What the blue-tailed ramshackled son of a seagoing *cocinero* you reckon I mean?" Whisk didn't wait for an answer. "You're damn right, the checker game! I got my next move all set in my head. No matter what way your Pa goes, I got him! I know I have!"

"Pa whupped you last six games in a row," Jess said.

Whisk glowered at him, then chuckled. "But I got him this time. I know it, sure as drought. Only it's your Pa's move, and I can't make mine till he's done his, and if he ain't back 'fore it's time to roll the coach out, I'll have to leave without I've played, and I *can't* do that. I just plain *can't!*"

Jess nodded.

"Well?" Whisk demanded.

"Well what?"

161

"What you gonna do about it?"

"Me?"

"Jesse, I can't wait for Deke. If he ain't back tomorrow, then somebody'll have to play for him, and you're the best hand with checkers in the whole brood. You'll have to —"

"Whoa! Hold on, Whisk. Pa'd peel my hide off for saddle strings if I was to play in his place."

Whisk snorted. Squinting at Jess, he said, "Looky, ain't you Wileys always talking how you're all one family and what one does is the same as any of you was to do it? Ain't you always saying that?"

Jess recollected he'd been thinking something of just that kind when he kissed Miss Lucinda Cummins of Fairwater, Virginia, on behalf of his brother. He had to admit, "I reckon."

"Then what's the difference? Why can't you move just this once for your Pa? It's rightful for you to do it, ain't it? Ain't it, boy?"

"Unh-ugh."

"Dammit, Jesse, I can't hold my water from here to next month. I got to make my play 'fore I pull out to the county seat again. I just *got* to!"

"I got things to do, too," Jess said. His frown had turned into cocked-brow speculation. "I tell you what, Whisk. I might trade you."

Whisk cocked a suspicious brow back at him. "Trade for what?"

"A favor. Won't cost you nothing, only a little time."

"Man my age ain't got much time to fritter

around with," Whisk said. "What kind of a favor?"

"You heard about how me and Hash Harker is gonna have a duel?"

"Sure have. Everybody this end of the county's heard by now. What you want from me?"

"Well," Jess drawled, "it's kinda this way. You see, Whisk, I got a problem."

"Problem, huh? Hell, you young sprouts these days ain't even got no notions what a problem is. I tell you, when I was your age, that was when we had us some real problems. I ever tell you about the time me and Jim Bridger was up to Raton Pass together and —"

"Yeah, you told me," Jess interrupted. He swung his leg back over the roan's withers and lifted rein. "I'll be seeing you, Whisk."

"What about the checker move!"

"What about my problem?"

"Hell! All right," the old man hollered at his back. "What's your problem?"

Jess halted the horse and swung it around so that he was facing Whisk again. "About the duel. It seems I kinda need somebody to second for me in it."

"Huh? Hell, boy, whyn't you say so? Is that what you want to trade. Me seconding you in your duel, and you playing your Pa's move?"

Jess nodded.

Whisk grinned. "I'd be right pleased. I ain't backed nobody up in a proper duel since old

Charlie the Frenchman shot the shirt stud off Gentleman Jeraboam over to Fort Whiskey Smith couple years after Appomattox. I'll say, boy, that sure was one dandy of a duel. Pair of horse pistols like steamboat stacks, belonged to the judge. Smooth bore. That's what you rightly use for dueling by the rules, you know. Gotta be smooth bore. Coulda loaded a whole keg of horseshoe nails down one of 'em. Fact, I think that's what Charlie done. I ever tell you about that duel, boy?"

"Lots of times."

"Likely I never told you the whole of it. You climb down, boy, set in the shade, and make your move, and I'll give her to you, both barrels."

"After my duel," Jess answered, lifting rein again.

"Looky, boy, you come on, set and play your move, and I'll tell you some dueling stories as'll have your hind teeth up on end."

"Later," Jess said, setting the roan into a lope.

"Jesse!" Whisk shouted after him. "Jesse, you ain't made your Pa's move!"

"Later!"

"When?"

"When the plans for my duel is settled."

"But . . . but . . ."

But Jess was a distance away now, and getting farther away every moment.

Planting his hands on his hips, Whisk worked up spit and let fly. As it hit ground, he heard hooves behind him. He turned just in time to miss being run down by July and Hassan on the pinto.

"Young'uns," he grunted, and spat again.

Junie, too, had recollected about the duel. And about the fight she'd had with Dominic last night. For a while she'd let it slip her mind that she was mad at him. Remembering, she glared at him and asked if he'd heard anything new about the affair.

Shrugging, he said, "Jesse ain't got him no second yet."

Jacob put in, "He was here a few minutes ago asking Dom to do it for him."

"And you turned him down, didn't you?" Junie's mouth tightened, and her voice hardened as her anger grew. "I know you did. You just don't care what I want, do you?"

"I care," Dominic tried weakly.

But she kept right on going. "You'll just stand around and watch and let Jesse and poor darling Hash just shoot each other to death without you lift a hand to stop it, won't you?"

"Junie, there ain't nothing I can do."

"Oh, hell!" she announced, turning her back on him. "I got a mind to walk right out on you."

Maybe that wouldn't be such a bad thing, he thought. He said, "If that's what you want."

Maybe it wouldn't be such a bad thing, she thought. She said, "I ought to go home to my Ma."

"Junie," Miss Lucinda slurred, "if you gonna leave him, why don' you come home with me? We can talk about . . . about . . . things."

"Huh?" Speculation sparked into Junie's eyes. She looked appraisingly at her new friend and thought of the possible advantages of staying awhile in Hash Harker's house.

Misreading her expression, Miss Lucinda said, "I got Mrs. Delphinia to chaperon. You stay with me. Mr. Harker won't mind. We can talk. Jesse and Jacob, they'll come see you, won't they?"

Junie slowly smiled.

"Wimmin," Dominic grunted. He stabbed his bar rag at the damp rings on the mahogany.

"A woman was the beginning of it all," the Reverend P. Jonathan Seven said, rising to address the group at the bar. "The lady Eve in the Garden of Eden began it when she enticed our poor ancestor, Adam, into partaking of the accursed *apple*."

"Pomegranate!" Ezekiel W. Trot shouted, jumping up.

"Apple," the Reverend said firmly.

Ezekiel W. Trot faced the group at the bar as if they were judge and jury, come to decide the matter. "It says right there in the good Book that the Garden of Eden was on the Euphrates River, don't it?"

He turned back to the Reverend and demanded, "Don't it?"

The Reverend nodded reluctantly.

"And there don't no apples grow around the

Euphrates River," Ezekiel W. Trot continued. "I learnt that from the lips of a real scholar sort of man who'd read the Good Book from one end to the other and back again, and had went to the Euphrates River on a boat to have him a look at the Garden of Eden for himself. There in the Turkish country, that's where! He walked his own feet right over the ground where the Garden of Eden stood and he seen it with his own eyes, and he said there ain't no *apples* grow around there at all. It's pomegranates!"

Devoutly, the Reverend P. Jonathan Seven quoted, " 'And the Lord God planted a garden eastward in Eden and there he put the man who he had formed. And out of the ground made the Lord God to grow every tree that is pleasant to the sight and good for *food*.' "

He glowered at Ezekiel W. Trot. "*Every* tree, you cussed old vinegarroon."

"Like *pomegranate* trees!"

"Like *apple* trees!"

"Pomegranate!"

"Apple!"

They faced each other across the table, their audience once more forgotten.

Junie turned to Miss Lucinda. "Let's us go on home."

"Your house or mine?"

"Yours," she said with a smile.

Miss Lucinda looked to Jacob. The corners of her mouth twisted. Misty stars staggered in her eyes.

Huskily she said, "Will you drive us home now, Jacob, honey?"

"Yes'm," he beamed.

Dominic sighed as he watched the three of them leave together, arm in arm. He poured himself another drink. Lifting his glass, he said, "To wimmin."

And grinned.

CHAPTER 15

The old Studebaker wagon had been painted green when it was new. Now it was faded to a dull gray. At the reins, January Wiley sat gazing into the distance. She had on her best calico dress, her good bonnet, and her boots. She was nervous. The idea of going partying always flustered her.

The rocking chair lay in the back of the wagon. Mrs. Deke sat beside her daughter. Her eyes were closed, and her hands were folded over the bottle of laudanum in her lap. Nothing ever flustered her.

January had swung the wagon off the wheel ruts from the Wiley place and was well onto the wagon road toward town when she spotted a rider coming toward her. She squinted suspiciously at him until she could make out that it was Jess on the blue roan.

He waved at her.

Halting the wagon, she waved back.

"Got yourself a second yet?" she asked as he reined up.

"Whisk Shaker," he told her. "Where you heading? The partying ain't set to start for hours yet."

"I know. I thought I'd pick up some more lau-

169

danum for Ma, and let her set sociable with Mrs. Grandly awhile 'fore it starts."

Jess gave her a hint of a grin. "Sure. You ain't really in a hurry to get where the fellers can see you all decked out in your partying dress."

January blushed red. Through her coating of cornstarch face powder and road dust, it showed as splotches of muddy pink.

"Jesse Wiley!" she protested. "Such a thing to say!"

"One of these days one of them fellers is gonna run off and take you away from us," he said.

She shook her head in denial and smiled at her brother. There was a touch of wistfulness in the smile.

"Where you heading?" she asked.

"Back to the house. Anything I can fetch for you?"

"No."

"Jesse, that you, son?" Mrs. Deke murmured. She lifted her lashes enough to peek out at him.

"Yes'm."

"You seen Mr. Wiley lately?"

"No'm."

"I don't know where that man's got off to this time," she said with a small puzzled frown. Mr. Wiley never used to go and leave her without he told her where he was going and gave her some notion when he figured to be back.

She glanced around. Her head tilted back, aiming her eyes skyward. She smiled then.

"There he is now."

Jess looked up.

The spread wings of the buzzard were silhouetted against the bright blue of the sky.

"Tell him to come on out to the partying," Mrs. Deke said. "Tell him I'll be waiting for him there."

"Yes'm." Jess nodded dutifully as he lifted rein.

"Take care, Jesse," January said. She clucked at the wagon horse. It leaned, lurching the old wagon into motion.

"You'll tell him, won't you, son?" Mrs. Deke called after Jess.

"Yes'm," he repeated, looking over his shoulder. The buzzard was still there, hanging above him in the sky.

He looked back again when he reached the Wiley house. And saw the buzzard again. He had no doubt that it was following him.

Pulling the roan up under the big pecan tree, he dropped the reins and swung himself onto the low limb. He seated himself on the remains of the tree house, with his elbows on his knees and his chin in his hands, and frowned at his thoughts.

He wasn't at all surprised when he saw a large dark shadow come skimming across the ground and halt just beyond his own. Leaves rustled as the buzzard lit in the tree over his head. He didn't look up at it.

Softly he said, "Who the hell are you, anyway?"

No answer.

He craned his neck around then, and squinted at the bird. It cocked its head, peering back at him through a sharp critical eye.

His Ma was right about that wrinkledy leathery old bald head, he thought. It did look an awful lot like Deke Wiley.

He asked it, "You really my Pa?"

Again, no answer.

He wondered if he actually expected one. But, hell, even that was like his old man. Deke Wiley could be just as silent stubborn and set on his own mind as any Arkansas jackrabbit.

"You're either Pa," he decided aloud, "or you're the devil come to fetch me."

The bird didn't so much as blink.

"Who the hell are you?" Jess said again. "Huh?"

July and Hassan waved as they passed the wagon with January and Mrs. Deke. They didn't stop. As they neared the house, July swung the pinto off to one side, so the edge of the porch cut her line of sight right up to the roan's tail. She was pretty sure Jess was up in the tree again. She hoped he hadn't seen her ride up.

Stopping by the porch, she nudged Hassan. He slipped off the pony's back, and she followed him down. They crept under the floor of the porch, into cool shadows infested by sleeping hounds.

Old Bugler bared a rheumy eye at them. He gave a drowsy tentative scratch in the general direction of a particularly annoying flea, then continued with his snoring.

On their hands and knees, July and Hassan looked out into the yard. The roan had trotted over to the corral. Jess was in the pecan tree. So was the buzzard.

"You reckon I ought to shoot him?" July whispered.

"Jesse?" Hassan asked with a start.

"No, you donkey. The buzzard."

"Oh."

"You reckon?"

"Not if he's really your Pa."

July nodded agreement. She watched Jess twist around to speak to the bird, then climb down from the tree and head for the kitchen.

After a moment Jess came back with his hands full of something. He held it up to the tree like an offering. It was a meat bone January had put aside for soup awhile back. Too far back. Even if the green growths were scraped off, it wouldn't have been fit for soup now.

"Pa?" he called uncertainly, eyeing the dark hulk among the pecan leaves.

The buzzard spread its wings. It hesitated with them outheld and one eye cocked toward Jess. Then it opened its maw. Barely seeming to move the huge wings, it tilted forward and glided down toward Jess.

He backstepped, holding the meat bone out at arm's length.

The buzzard snatched with its talons. It

caught the bone, gave a couple of flaps of its wings, rose, and flew on. Just past the barn, it dropped the bone and lit beside it.

Hooking his thumbs in his pockets, Jess stood and watched as the bird began to peck at the bone.

July squirmed from under the porch, with Hassan close behind her. She hurried to her brother's side. He gave her a quick sidelong glance, as if he'd been expecting her all the while, and was surprised she hadn't got here till now, then returned his brooding attention to the buzzard.

"Is that really our Pa?" July asked him.

He shrugged. "Damned if I know."

Mrs. Grandly's Family Boardinghouse was a big adobe building with a false frame front that included a covered porch lined with wicker rockers. It was situated on Main Street not far from the coach stable. With the exception of a couple of cantinas near the border that catered to Mexicans and fast-moving men who tended to travel light and sleep by day, it provided the only regular accommodations and meals for travelers in this end of the county. Even so, business was seldom brisk. Several townsfolk made their home at the boardinghouse, but at present only one traveler was in residence, and he had come to Hardly by mistake.

Weston Finlay wanted to go to Arizona Territory. He hoped to go there as soon as possible.

All his life, Weston had considered himself to be of a particularly weak constitution. During his years with Slattery's Superior Specialties, he had heard an endless exposition of the symptoms to be treated by Old Doc Slattery's Superior Soothing Syrup and had discovered himself to be suffering from each and every one.

After the untimely death of Mrs. Finlay (formerly Miss Felicity Slattery), he found himself with an excellent annual income from his considerable inheritance, and he was free to seek a more salubrious clime than Newark, New Jersey. He had set out for Bitter Drip, Arizona, where it was said the air was most marvelously restorative, the water unpalatably curative, and the local Indians adept in the secret arts of herbs and simples. There he intended to spend his declining years, preferably with a hardy, self-reliant, yet tender and loving woman of good pioneer stock to minister to his needs.

Now he wasn't sure he had any declining years ahead of him. He was certain the road agent he'd encountered first at the coach holdup and then in the tonsorial parlor meant to take his life.

Behind the bolted door of his rented bedroom, he morosely contemplated his past, his present, and his prospects for a future. Could it all end like this?

The knock on his door startled him almost as much as the confrontation with the bandit in the barbershop had. But the voice that followed the knock was Mrs. Grandly's.

The goodly landlady'd heard what happened in the barbershop. She understood why Mr. Finlay had come dashing through the parlor in his shirtsleeves a short while before. Being a kindly woman, with motherly feelings toward everyone, she'd come to Weston's door with a cup of rum-coffee for him, and assurances that he really had nothing to fear from any of the Wiley boys.

Weston was appreciably calmed by her soothing words and her rum-coffee. He allowed himself to be lured out of the bedroom. He even went so far as to return to the tonsorial parlor to collect his coat and pay his bill. Returning, he joined Mrs. Grandly on the porch.

They were sitting side by side discussing Hardly, the West in general, the Wileys in particular, and whatever else came to mind, when the old Studebaker wagon rolled to a halt at the front steps. The two people in the wagon looked to be of the feminine gender. Being a man of manners and properly conditioned reflexes, Weston rose from his rocker and went to offer them assistance down from the high wagon seat.

Both women wore poke bonnets. When the one who held the reins turned to look at him, he found himself peering into the deep tunnel of the sunshade, seeing nothing beyond the tip of a nose but darkness.

The hand that accepted his was young and strong, callused and worn with hard work. The woman, when she stepped down, proved to be a

176

head taller than Weston. A long, lean, lanky woman with the suggestion of good sturdy bone and sinewy muscle under her simple calico frock.

The late Mrs. Finlay had been short and, when first wed, pleasingly plump. By the time she passed on, she was downright fat. It had taken the embalmer, the dresser, and the funeral director himself, all working with wedges, to cram her into the fancy bronze casket. During the years of her increase and decline, her husband had developed an intense dislike for female flesh in large quantities.

The woman he faced now was, to his delight, the antithesis of the late Mrs. Finlay.

This, he thought, was truly a perfect example of the hardy enduring breed of woman born of the elemental wilderness of the frontier.

January appreciated the hand down from the wagon. But now she was standing on the ground with no more need of help, and this strange little man in the derby was still clutching her fingers. She didn't know what to do. She thought she ought to say something. A *thankee,* maybe. That seemed like the proper polite sort of thing to say in such a situation. But the word got jammed up in her throat.

She peered down the deep tube of her sunbonnet at the face that gazed up at her. He had brown eyes. Sad, soulful brown eyes an awful lot like old Bugler's, though not nearly so old and rheumy-looking. She had a notion that a man with such eyes must be in bad need of a good woman to take care of him.

She blushed at her thoughts.

At last she found some words she could speak. "Gimme a hand down with my Ma, will you, mister?"

"My pleasure, madam," he said, bowing slightly. He was still holding onto her hand. "Or is it 'miss'?"

"M-m-miss," she said. It never occurred to her to give him her name.

He recognized her shyness as unfeigned. He found it most becoming.

Together they hefted Mrs. Deke down from the wagon and up the steps to the porch, where they gently deposited her in the rocker next to Mrs. Grandly.

" 'Afternoon, Mrs. Deke," Mrs. Grandly said.

" 'Afternoon, Mrs. Grandly," Mrs. Deke said.

The rockers creaked, not quite in unison.

Mrs. Grandly raised her cup. Pausing before she drank, she asked, "Speck of coffee, Mrs. Deke?"

Mrs. Deke raised her laudanum bottle. "Thankee, no, I brung my soothing syrup."

"Ma," January said, "I'm going down, fetch you some more laudanum. Be back in a few minutes."

"That's nice," Mrs. Deke said.

Weston Finlay asked, "May I accompany you?"

January started. Again, she was at a loss for

words. She could feel herself blushing. With a nod, she wheeled away from Weston and hurried to the wagon. Leading the horse, she started toward the pharmacy.

Weston fell in beside her. He wondered why she was taking the wagon along. At the pharmacy, his curiosity was satisfied. She hadn't come for merely a bottle or two of soothing syrup, but for an entire case of it. Not Doc Slattery's, though, he noticed. He thought it might be well worthwhile to try switching her to the Slattery brand if she bought in such quantity often.

The laudanum was in a huge wooden crate with a rope handle on each end. The pharmacist, who proved to be the same well-spoken, dark-complexioned gentleman he'd seen in the tonsorial parlor, took one handle. The young woman reached for the other.

Weston protested. Although she was obviously stronger, sturdier, and more accustomed to such heavy work than he, he felt himself bound by custom and by the desire to make a good impression on her. He insisted on carrying her end of the crate.

She seemed astonished by his offer. Bewildered, she stepped aside and let him take the handle.

By the time the crate was settled next to the rocking chair in the back of the wagon, Weston was gasping for breath and dripping perspiration. He leaned against the tailgate lest he collapse, and wrung his flushed, aching hands.

The woman peered down the length of her bonnet at him. "Why, you're plumb tuckered out."

"I'm not a well man," he said, his shoulders heaving with each effort for breath.

"I *knowed* it!" She lost her shyness in a surge of sympathy. "I just knowed it when I looked into them eyes of yours. I knowed you was a troubled, suffering creature."

"You did?" Weston perked with enthusiasm. He seldom met anyone who showed recognition of the true depths of his constitutional deficiencies.

"Sure," she said. "Here, lemme help you up on the wagon. We'll ride back to the boarding-house."

"I do appreciate your gentle thoughtfulness," he answered, taking the hand she held out. He leaned heavily on her arm as she hoisted him toward the wagon seat. A good, strong arm, he thought.

She clambered up next to him and lifted the reins. Eyeing him through the tunnel of her bonnet, she suggested tentatively, "It might be a bit of fresh air'd help."

"I could certainly use some."

"Reckon we might ride around town a ways 'fore we go back."

"It would be a great pleasure," he said with a wan smile.

Though he couldn't see it for the bonnet, she

smiled back at him. Her nervousness was completely gone. All of her thoughts were concerned with this little man who was so obviously so badly in need of the tender care of a good woman.

CHAPTER 16

The vulture was still nibbling at the meat bone when Jess decided it was time for him to get going to Hash Harker's party. The bird kept pecking away at the bone, watching him askance as he switched his saddle from the roan to a gray geld.

July had fed her pinto some corn and rubbed down its legs. Now she and the pony and Hassan were waiting together outside the corral.

When Jess led out the gray and mounted up, she asked him, "Leaving?"

He nodded.

"For the partying?"

He nodded again. "You going?"

"Uh-huh."

"I reckon you're looking to ride over with me?"

"No."

"You ain't?"

"We'll be along later," she told him.

He understood. She'd sooner track his trail than ride beside him. He gave her a quick grin and nudged the gray into an amble.

The buzzard had one foot planted on the bone and was tugging at a particularly tough shred of meat. Looking back over his shoulder at it, Jess said, "You coming?"

The bird cocked an eye at him and went on tugging.

He felt a mite foolish talking to a buzzard in front of July and Hassan, but then neither of them wasn't sure the thing wasn't the spirit of Deke Wiley either. And he had made a promise to his mother.

Dutifully he called, "Ma says you should come on out to the partying. She'll be waiting for you there."

The buzzard bobbed its head.

Frowning, Jess studied on whether it had replied to what he'd said, or had just pulled a bit of meat loose of the bone. He couldn't decide. He kept on staring at the bird.

It lifted its head to look directly at him. Stretching its scrawny neck, it opened its maw wide.

If it meant something by that, he couldn't figure out what. Shrugging to himself, he tapped his spurs against the gray's sides. The horse stepped into a lope, and he swung it toward the wagon road.

Behind him, July and Hassan scrambled up onto the pinto's bare back. They sat awhile, switching glances from Jess to the buzzard and back again. The gray was almost out of sight before July kicked up the pinto and set out after her brother.

The vulture took another nip at the bone. It was almost bare now. Giving a kick that sent it

skittering across the yard, the bird launched itself into the air and set off after the pinto.

Hash Harker's house was just east of Hardly.
It was set back at the far end of a drive lined with
scraggly young cottonwoods meant to resemble
the old oaks lining drives to fine mansions in the
plantation country.

The house was built of red brick that had been
freighted in. So was the carriage house, and even
the backhouse. Some folks were mighty im-
pressed by that. Others considered it ostenta-
tious.

The party was being held in the yard. At this
time of year, there was no threat of rain, but the
wind could come up strong at sunset, so paulins
had been stretched from poles along two sides of
the partying ground for windbreaks. Ropes
strung from pole to pole supported lanterns of
all kinds and colors, including a few of the fancy
Oriental sort, supplied by Dominic Johanssen
from his personal collection for this very special
occasion.

Dominic was catering the drinks, but the
womenfolk were showing off their skills by
bringing the food. A row of trestle tables with
bedsheets for tablecloths were quickly filling up
with victuals.

Half-kegs served for punch bowls, and for
them who found punch too tame, there were
straight bottled goods at a makeshift bar which
Dominic insisted on tending. He was willing to

pour freely for one and all, but he refused to leave the bottles for folks to help themselves. He was afraid too many of them would help themselves to whole bottles at a time, stowing them away in saddle pockets and under wagon seats to be consumed at their own convenience.

The carriage house served as a repository for saddles and firearms. A flatbed wagon, pulled up against one wall, served as a stage for the band. When Jess arrived, the musicians were together on the wagon, tuning up.

Matt Matthews was pulling long cat howls out of the fiddle he held tucked in the crook of his arm. At his side, Mrs. Grandly squeezed similiar wails out of her concertina.

The instrument was part of her legacy from her first husband, the one prior to the late Mr. Grandly. He'd been a salt-sea sailor and had disappeared in pursuit of an eighty-barrel right whale off Greenland, leaving her the concertina, several hand-carved fish-ivory busks, a daguerreotype of himself in a frock coat and stovepipe hat, and a curious bone soup spoon reputed to have been carved from the thighbone of a South Pacific cannibal king. She never used the spoon, but she wore the busks regularly, kept the daguerreotype on her mantelpiece, and pumped the concertina whenever there was a fancy affair around Hardly, which was hardly ever.

The Peckett boys — Pike, Pete, and Dacey — were noodling around on their Jew's harps, waiting for the first number to begin. Abe Washington Grant was hurriedly replacing the fifth string on his homemade squirrel-skin banjo. Juan Orlando was bending his head low over his guitar, playing softly, scowling intently as his long slender fingers danced over the strings. Completing the ensemble were Ali Ibn with the bass jug and Dawn Woman on drums.

In front of the bandstand, several squares were made up, waiting for the music to begin. The folks who weren't going to dance were helping themselves to food, wandering around, or sitting on the chairs and benches along two sides of the partying ground.

Jess halted the gray near the carriage house. From the saddle he scanned the crowd. He spotted his mother in her rocker under a huge Chinese lantern with long yellow tassels that rippled in the breeze. Mrs. Deke rocked slowly fro and to, her eyes half-closed, her hands clamping her laudanum bottle to her body. A small smile lay comfortably on her face.

He picked out Junie and Jacob in one of the squares. They stood side by side, paying no attention to each other. Junie was gazing across the square at Hash Harker. Jacob grinned at Miss Lucinda, who waited by Harker. She darted coy glances back at him.

Nance and Jody stood together in the same square, leaning shoulder against shoulder and hip against hip, oblivious of everyone but themselves.

The fourth couple in the square gave Jess a start. The woman in the sunbonnet was his very own sister January, and the man at her side was the one in the derby who'd come in on the coach yesterday.

Weston Finlay considered himself somewhat frail for such festivities as this, but when the woman in the bonnet asked him along, he'd felt he could hardly decline such a charming and gracious invitation from such a charming and sympathetic person. When she'd proposed that he dance with her, he'd agreed, happily anticipating the opportunity to hold her beautifully callused hand and to slip his arm around her wonderfully slender waist.

But as the square made up, he had suddenly found himself surrounded by two of the men who'd stopped the stagecoach. He'd been too upset to do more than stand gawking while the young woman calmly introduced the two as her brothers Jacob and Jody.

To Weston's amazement, each brother had heartily shaken his hand, welcoming him to the town and the party.

Now he leaned limply against Miss January Wiley, feeling as if fate had brought him through some perilous adventure. He felt he'd been spared the wrath of the Wiley boys for a particular purpose. He had been destined to come to Hardly, to this very moment, to find Miss January Wiley. And now that he had found her, he meant to hold on to her forever.

187

Matt Matthews drew a final mournful wail from his fiddle. He tapped the bow on the edge of the instrument for attention. The other instruments ceased their grunting, hooting, and whining. The crowd fell expectantly silent.

From somewhere behind the carriage house, a lone voice rang out, "Pomegranate!"

It was answered, "Apple!"

Matt began to count, slapping the sole of his boot on the wagonbed with each beat. "Uh-one, uh-two, uh-three . . ."

The music began.

Sawing at his fiddle, Matt started to chant the calls. "Bow to your partner, bow to your corner . . ."

The squares bounced into motion.

". . . All join hands and circle 'round."

Each square became a ring, a wheel rim turning. One circle broke suddenly. A figure darted away from it, cutting helter-skelter through the patterns of the dance.

Waving his bandaged arm as he ran, Whisk Shaker shouted, "Jesse! Jesse Wiley!"

Behind him, the wheels continued to turn.

Jess waved back and dismounted to meet him.

"I brung the game board," Whisk puffed as he reached Jess. "I got it all set up over to the end of the pie table. All you got to do now is just make your move."

"You got the duel all set up yet?" Jess asked.

"Everything except only what time it'll be at.

Come on, Jesse, you promised you'd make the move."

"I promised I'd do it after the duel was all arranged."

"It is all arranged. Just but the time."

"That's the most important thing. I want to know when it's gonna happen."

"Oh, hell," Whisk grumbled. "All right. You got a particular notion when you want it to be at?"

"I'd like to get it over with right soon."

"Me too! Whenever time me and Jacob agree on, that's all right with you, eh?"

"Yeah," Jess said.

Whisk dashed back into the patterns of dancers. As he came up to Jacob, Matt called a do-si-do. Whisk folded his arms and fell in at Jacob's side, following along, talking eagerly.

Jess unsaddled the gray and let it into the rope corral that had been set up to accommodate visiting horses. He deposited his saddle and hand gun inside the carriage house. As he was coming out, July and Hassan rode up. They waved at him.

As he waved back, he saw the buzzard. It was silhouetted against the twilight sky. He watched it arrive and settle on the ridge of the carriage-house roof.

It peered down at him.

Hooking his thumb toward the row of chairs on the far side of the dancers, he looked up at it and said, "Ma's over there."

Mrs. Deke was rocking slowly, smiling contentedly. She saw the party through her lowered lashes as swirls of color. She heard the music as waves of happiness. Someone had put a piece of peach pie into one of her hands. Whenever she remembered it, she took a bite.

Mrs. Grandly, who'd been sitting beside her for a while, had gone off somewhere, leaving the next rocker empty. Mrs. Deke wished someone would come set in it and keep her company.

Across the way, Mrs. Delphinia Quick (widowed) stood alone in the midst of the crowd watching the dancers. Her stays were laced too snugly and her very stylishly pointed patent leather boots were too tight. She was weary. Her long journey escorting Miss Lucinda to Hardly had been tiring. Much of her life had been tiring. She wished she could take off the shoes, undo the laces, and rest. But custom forbade such luxuries in public. She hoped for little more than to find a place to sit down.

She spotted an empty rocker over under a big Chinese lantern. She picked her way through the crowd and lowered her bulk into the chair. As her weight left her feet, she sighed with relief.

Enviously, she noticed that the old woman in the chair beside her seemed to be asleep. She knew it would be most unseemly for one of her own social standing to fall asleep in public, but she thought perhaps, just this once, now that she had completed her mission and delivered her charge safely to the prospective bridegroom, she might relax, if only for a short while.

She stretched out her legs under her skirts, leaned back her head, and considered the possibility of dozing. She was just closing her eyes when the old woman at her side surprised her by speaking to her.

In a soft and kindly voice, Mrs. Deke said, "Care for a sip of soothing syrup?"

Mrs. Delphinia Quick surprised herself even more by replying, "I don't mind if I do."

Mrs. Deke held out the bottle. Mrs. Delphinia took a swallow from it. She hadn't tasted soothing syrup for years. The tang of it brought to mind Professor Marvel. She hadn't thought of him for years.

Ever since she'd taken up residence in Fairwater, Virginia, Mrs. Delphinia Quick (widowed) had been telling people that she was formerly the wife of a noted Confederate officer, and the daughter of an aristocratic Southern landholder. She'd told of the family plantation being destroyed in the war, of the late Colonel Quick being valiantly slain in action, and of the carpetbaggers driving her family into ruin. She'd detailed her own trials in establishing herself in a position not intolerable to a gentlewoman of her breeding. She'd told the same stories so often for so long that at times she believed them herself.

But now the soft strength of the laudanum was stirring up memories that had lain buried at the bottom of her mind for many years. She contem-

plated them, first with uncertainty, then with af-
fection.

Over the distance of time, she discovered that
she was homesick for the shabby pine-slab
shanty where she'd been born. She missed her
eight barefoot brothers and three barefoot sisters
in their tattered hand-me-downs. She missed
her own barefoot childhood self. There had been
no laces and stays and bunion-pinching boots,
or soul-pinching social conventions, in those
days.

Sideways, Mrs. Deke eyed the woman next to
her. She didn't think she'd seen this one before.
She asked, "New to these parts?"

"Yes, I am Hash Harker's house guest," Mrs.
Delphinia announced in reply.

"That's nice. I'm Mrs. Deke Wiley."

"I am Mrs. Delphinia Quick, widowed, of
Fairwater, Virginia."

"I'm pleasured to meet you."

"The pleasure is mine," Mrs. Delphinia said
as she accepted the bottle Mrs. Deke offered
again. She drank deeply, savoring the soothing
syrup. Already, she was feeling its comfortable
warmth through her body.

"A most tasty potion," she said.

"Mr. Ali Ibn mixes it up for me special. Have
some more?"

"Thank-you. You are most neighborly, Mrs.
Wiley."

"Call me Missus Deke. Everybody else
does."

"You may call me Missus Delphinia."

"That's nice."

"It was my mother's name," Mrs. Delphinia said. She missed her mother. And the sisters with whom she had shared all her secrets as a child. It had been a long time since there was anyone she could confide in freely. She sighed with the weariness of having held so many secrets so tightly for so long. It was worse than being laced in stays.

Mrs. Deke held out the laudanum again. Mrs. Delphinia drank again. Returning the bottle, she said, "This is even better than Professor Marvel's Pure Herbal Remedy."

After a moment of consideration, Mrs. Deke said, "Can't say as how I recall that flavor."

"I don't expect it's still being made," Mrs. Delphinia told her. "It was a special formula of the professor's own. He died a right while back."

"Not painful, I hope."

"Hanged."

"Oh."

"A real shame. The professor was such a nice man. He came around with his medicine show back when I was very young. Just turning woman. That was the first time I ever tasted soothing syrup." Suddenly Mrs. Delphinia giggled to herself. A bright recollection glistened in her eyes. She leaned toward Mrs. Deke and confided, "I ran off with him."

"That's nice," Mrs. Deke said.

"He taught me a lot of things. He's the one

who taught me to shuffle and deal cards."

"My man, Mr. Wiley, he can turn a fair card. Leastways, he used to. Don't know if he can now, with them old claws for fingers." Mrs. Deke turned a slow glance toward the buzzard perched on the roof of the carriage house.

The gentle warmth of the laudanum and of revived memories had breached the barriers of propriety Mrs. Delphinia had so carefully constructed over the years. As they crumbled away, she continued, "After the professor, there was Nicholas Cresspool. He was a real gentleman. A remittance man from England. Suffolk, I think he said. Fine old family. He taught me proper ladylike ways, and I taught him the cards. We got along fine together. Until he was shot over a hand of stud poker."

Sympathetically, Mrs. Deke offered her more laudanum.

She took a deep draft. It was truly a very fine potion. She felt as much at ease now as if she'd loosed all her laces. She gave the bottle back and went on talking.

"It wasn't exactly *over* the cards that he was shot. Was right through them. The bullet pierced the ten of diamonds and his left lung. He lingered just long enough to sign all his property over to me. Didn't have anything from his family. Youngest son, you know. But he'd won a lot with his gambling. Over three thousand dollars just that night. Set me up in Fairwater, Virginia, as a proper lady. Been one ever since."

"That's nice," Mrs. Deke said, holding out the bottle again.

"It was real fine," Mrs. Delphinia answered after she'd taken another drink. "For a while. But a body grows weary of being a fine lady, always putting on style for everybody. Never letting loose and being plain old you. There's times I'd like to up and really let go. Kick off my shoes and cuss like my maw used to. Lordy, a woman can get tired of being laced up in stays all the time."

"Never wear them myself," Mrs. Deke murmured.

Mrs. Delphinia rolled her eyes in envy. Her eyelids felt very heavy. She had a notion she might nap soon, maybe after one more sip of laudanum. She no longer cared what people thought.

She said, "That's nice."

CHAPTER 17

The evening sun was hanging heavy over the horizon, its face turning red and its light stretching long fingers of shadow around the folk at the partying, but nobody paid it any mind. Tonight even the chickens would be staying up late.

The band sawed merrily away at "Old Joe Clark." They and the dancers had got up a good head of steam and were going strong. All were of a mood to keep going until exhaustion set in.

When the music suddenly stopped, the silence was startling. The dancers, in the middle of a promenade, stopped. They looked at each other and then at the band.

Whisk Shaker had finally succeeded in dragging Jacob out of his square and up onto the stage. Jacob stood grinning proudly at everybody. Whisk, at his side, looked as happy as a pig in a mash heap. He waved his arms for attention. He needn't have bothered. He already had every eye in the crowd, excepting those of the Reverend P. Jonathan Seven and Ezekiel W. Trot, who were still carrying on their conversation behind the carriage house.

"Folks," Whisk announced, "you all know Hash Harker and Jesse Wiley is gonna have a duel, and Jacob here and me is gonna second for them."

A loud delighted cheer went up.

"Well, to save all you folks from off in the county and the next counties over and you what's come up from Mexico special for this partying another long trip into Hardly, we're gonna have the duel tonight, in the morning, here at dawn."

Another cheer went up, this one even louder and more delighted.

Whisk scrambled down from the stage and shoved his way through the applauding crowd toward Jess.

"Now!" he hollered. "Now, are you satisfied? Come make your move."

"Dawn?" Jess said.

"That's right. That soon enough for you?"

"I reckon."

"Then, come on, dammit!" Whisk tugged at Jess's shirt sleeve. "Come on, make your move!"

"All right," Jess sighed. He glanced around. He spotted what he was looking for on the carriage-house roof. The vulture was perched there, staring down at the partying. If it was Deke, he thought, it sure wouldn't miss seeing him make the move. He hoped he wouldn't disappoint it.

The band had started up again where it left off, but nobody was dancing now. If anybody at the partying hadn't heard about the checker game, somebody was busy telling him. The rest of the crowd was following along behind Jess and Whisk, eager to see the move.

Jess could hear the murmuring behind him. Folks were making new bets and adding to old ones. He thought he ought to put a few dollars on the game himself. It was only sporting for a man to back himself. But somehow he just didn't feel the inclination.

The game was already set up over at the far end of the pie table. There were folks bunched around it, studying it, speculating on the potential moves, when Jess and Whisk came up. Falling silent, the spectators drew back to give Jess and Whisk thinking room.

Red and black, circles and squares. Jess frowned down at them. He already had a notion of the move he'd make, but he wasn't anxious to do it. He wanted to consider awhile longer. He wanted to feel certain in himself that he was doing the right thing.

The band had quit and hurried over to join the audience. The only sound was of the wind in the trees. A horse snuffled. Someone took a deep breath. His neighbors shushed him.

Jess thought he saw a really good move. But as his hand started toward his piece, he realized it would lead inevitably into a trap.

The next likely-looking move he considered worked out much the same way. He nibbled at his lower lip as he pondered the game.

Whisk stood across from him, grinning with anticipation.

In the crowd, Pecos Pike Griswald nudged Red Velasquez and whispered something. Red thought on it a moment, then whispered a reply. Pecos Pike shook his head in denial. Red gestured with his hands. The folk immediately around them scowled at the distraction and made small hissing sounds, demanding silence.

At last Jess reached a decision. He had a good move that looked completely safe. It wouldn't gain him anything in particular, but it shouldn't lose him anything either. That would be the best thing to do, he figured. Just stall the game for a play.

He put the tip of his forefinger on a piece.

The silence deepened. Not one of the spectators so much as breathed.

Jess shoved the man precisely into the next square over.

Silence.

Anticipation.

Whisk stood taut, his eyes narrowed, his reaching hand almost trembling. He touched a piece. He moved it.

With a solemn grin, he demolished his opponent completely.

Gasps.

Cheers.

Red and Pecos Pike pumped each other's hands as if they'd been the participants. Nettie Amberhurst pulled off her feathered bonnet and stomped on it. Jenny Bloch squeezed the baby girl she held in her arms so tight that the poor lit-

tle thing set to squawling. Gil Nash began to holler for the people whose bets he held to come pay
off.

Whisk sighed. His knees quivered. Gave way.
He found himself on his rump on the ground,
laughing violently.

Offering him a hand up, Jess said, "I reckon
I'm whupped."

Whisk waved away the offer. He sat there and
struggled for breath. When he finally got enough
to power a few words, he said, "Next game,
Jesse. Always a next game. You can start it
whenever you want."

Jess nodded and returned his grin.

Whisk accepted the helping hand then. He got
himself onto his feet and stood tottering. As he
brushed at his breeches, he said, "Look at that
old buzzard up there. Ornery-looking old cuss,
ain't it?"

Jess looked at the vulture. He nodded agreement and wondered whether it was a trick of the
light or whether the bird was scowling with disgust.

Under the pie table, hidden by the bedsheet
that had been pressed into service as a tablecloth, July and Hassan nibbled at the roast
chicken they'd borrowed from the next table
over and consulted on the situation.

"Jesse lost," July whispered dolefully.

Hassan's mouth was full. He mumbled unintelligibly and nodded.

"It could be an omen," she said.

He eyed her, swallowed, and said, "You think so?"

"I just ain't sure. Hassan, we got to do something about this here duel."

"What?"

"I ain't got it figured out yet. Lemme think on it awhile."

He nodded again and busied himself with a drumstick.

After a moment July shifted onto her hands and knees. As she started to squirm out from under the table, she said, "You wait here. I'll be back."

The band had reassembled and struck up a new tune. The dancers were back at work, tromping joyfully through a grand-right-and-left. Junie was among them, but she was moving automatically. Her thoughts were darkly occupied. She supposed she was going to have to do something about the impending duel herself.

Last night she'd noticed a brown pottery jug among the fancy decanters on the sideboard in Hash Harker's parlor, and she'd recognized it. Her Pa had brought a dozen of them up from Mexico awhile back, all filled with a special brew of mescal the like of which nobody around Hardly had ever tasted before. A brew as strong as a Spanish bull and as smooth as buckwheat honey. Deke had traded off four jugs and finished off the other eight with his family.

201

Junie reckoned the jug in Hash's parlor might be the only one left in the county with anything in it. She excused herself from the dance and hurried to the house. Sneaking surreptitiously through the twilight shadows, she fetched the jug and an empty decanter and headed for her family's wagon. She'd seen the case of laudanum in the wagon when January drove up, and it gave her ideas.

Using a broken knife that had been lying under the seat for the past few years, she pulled a couple of nails out of the top of the crate, then pried up the loosened board. She took the laudanum bottle from the corner of the box and emptied it into the decanter.

The pottery jug was about half full. She refilled the laudanum bottle from it, and returned the bottle to the crate. Then she emptied the decanter into the jug. The mixture was now at least two-thirds laudanum. Leaving the decanter lie, she set the board back in place on the crate, stoppered the jug, and set out to Dominic's makeshift bar.

He was busy setting up drinks. When she finally caught his eye, she told him, "You're gonna do something for me."

"What?" he said.

"Don't you go asking things as ain't none of your business. You just do what I tell you, you hear?"

He considered saying no, but he said yes.

Junie slipped him the jug. "You serve Jesse

and Hash out of this. Not nobody else. Just Jesse and Hash. And you make sure betwixt them they drink it all. You hear?"

Dominic nodded, shrugged, and accepted the jug. It made sense to him that she'd want Hash and her brother to enjoy the pleasures of the fine mescal before they faced each other over loaded pistols. He agreed with the idea.

Grinning slyly to herself, Junie hurried to rejoin the dancers. But the square she'd been in before had completely disintegrated. Jody and Nance had disappeared. So had January and Weston Finlay.

A small creek flowed off a ways behind the Harker house. Scrawny willows and cottonwoods struggled to survive along its banks. As the last red memories of day died in the western sky, January and Weston walked hand in hand among the trees.

"Mr. Finlay," January said. "I — uh — I've got a kinda problem."

"I shall do all within my power to assist you in its solution, Miss January," he replied. He hoped it was entirely an intellectual problem, not one requiring physical effort.

"It's about my brother Jesse. This duel he's gonna be in. I'm fearful he might get hurt. If he was to get hurt, I'd have to stay here and tend him till he was well again."

"We must not let him get hurt," Weston said gallantly.

"I got a notion what we might do about it," she told him.

"What?"

"Well, if Hash was to get hurt before the duel, just hurt a little bit, like maybe shot in the foot, that'd stop the whole affair, wouldn't it?"

"It certainly should."

January hesitated, then said, "I think I got to shoot Hash Harker."

"What!"

"Only just a little bit. I'll aim below the knee. I won't hurt him, only enough to stop him of dueling."

"Miss January!"

Weston was shocked. He was incredulous. He wondered if he could possibly be hearing what he heard.

"Here's the thing," January continued. "I ain't the best hand with a gun that there is. I might miss him the first shot or two. I got to have him off away from the crowd, lest I up and hurt somebody else by accident."

She was warming to her plan. Her voice filled with enthusiasm. She gestured broadly with the hand that Weston wasn't holding. "You can fetch him out here. I'll hide in the bushes yonder and put a bullet into his leg, and everything will be just fine. You will help me, Mr. Finlay?"

He could feel strength in the hand he held, and he could sense confidence in January's every move. He heard it in her voice. His uncertainty reluctantly yielded before her.

"Yes," he said, to his own dismay.

January smiled at him and tugged his hand. "Come on, let's get at it!"

Feeling numbly uneasy, he hurried along at her side.

Jacob and Whisk walked side by side toward the makeshift bar. They had been discussing the duel. Jacob had promised Junie he wouldn't let either Jess or Hash get bad hurt. He hoped Whisk could suggest something he might do.

Whisk had suggested they have a drink and think on it some. That struck Jacob as an excellent idea.

Stepping up to the bar, Jacob spotted the jug. He grunted with delight as he recognized it. "Dom! You got some of that there powerful mescal!"

"Uh-huh," Dominic responded, sounding a mite unsociable. He stuck the jug out of sight under the bar.

"Ain't you gonna give me none?" Jacob was shocked at such behavior.

Dominic shook his head.

"Ain't we always been friends?"

"Yeah," Dominic said sadly. He was embarrassed at having to refuse his friends the mescal jug. "I promised Junie I wouldn't give none of that to nobody but Jesse and Hash."

"Hell, Dom, just a little bit." Jacob measured off about an inch of air between his thumb and forefinger.

"I wish you wouldn't ask me. I done promised Junie."

"For Jesse and Hash, huh? On account of the duel?"

"I reckon."

"I'm in the same duel as them. Shouldn't I ought to get some, too?"

"No."

"Aw, Dom."

"No!"

"Jacob," Whisk said, tugging at Jacob's sleeve. "Come 'ere."

"Huh?"

"Just come here a minute."

"Unh." Jacob let himself be pulled away from the bar.

Whisk whispered into his ear. Jacob slowly grinned, then nodded and said, "Yeah!"

Whisk waited while Jacob ambled back to the bar and began to talk to Dominic again. Once Dominic was engrossed in the conversation, Whisk crept toward him. Flanking him, Whisk reached the bar, wrapped a hand around the jug, and crept back out again.

He and Jacob met by the Wiley wagon.

Whisk held up the jug in one hand and the empty decanter Junie had discarded in the other. The moon flashed pale bits of light from the faceted glass.

"Look what Providence up and provided for us," he said.

"That's purty. What we need it for?" Jacob asked.

"You'll see. Just you get that crate of soothing syrup open."

Jacob was pleased to find one board on top of the crate already loose. He pulled it off and took out the corner bottle while Whisk emptied the jug into the decanter. Together they refilled the jug with the contents of the laudanum bottle.

They returned the empty bottle to the crate and slid the loose plank back into place. Jacob took custody of the decanter, promising to wait for Whisk down by the creek. Whisk took the jug and stealthily returned it to the bar while Dominic was chatting with Pecos Pike and Red over a cup of corn doubles.

Pleased with his success, he hurried toward the creek to meet Jacob and the decanter.

Grinning with pleasure at her success, July slithered back under the pie table. She was carrying half a chocolate layer cake in one hand and something clutched tight in the other.

She handed Hassan the cake and lifted an edge of the tablecloth for light. Her clenched fist opened to show Hassan twelve pellets of lead that glistened with fresh nicks.

"Jesse left his sidearm in the carriage house, and Hash's was in his house hall," she said proudly. "Wasn't no trouble at all."

"It's their bullets?"

"Of course."

He frowned and asked, "How come you only took the lead instead of the whole cartridges? We coulda used them."

"I didn't do this for *us*. Done it for *them*. You reckon they wouldn't notice if their guns was empty? I had to leave them something as would go bang. Took the lead out and plugged up the ends of the cartridges with wax. They'll go off, all right, same as regular cartridges, only they won't shoot nobody."

Hassan eyed her with an admiration she felt she rightly deserved. She slipped the lead into the folds of her dress, figuring she'd find use for it later.

"Everything's going to be all right," she said. She gestured toward the cake Hassan held. "Let's us eat."

Everything was going all wrong, Miss Lucinda Cummins of Fairwater, Virginia, told herself as she do-si-doed around Hash Harker. She had to find some way of preventing the terrible bloodshed that was to be done in the name of her honor. She had to stop it at any cost.

"All change partners and swing that gal," Matt Matthews called.

A young man with a curly red beard and gapped teeth reached for Miss Lucinda. Evading him, she grabbed Hash's arm and pulled. He let her draw him away from the dance.

Off by the salad table, she faced him. Her brow puckered with determination and her chin lifted nobly. She spoke in a gush of words.

"Mr. Harker, I have given my promise to marry you, and I shall not break that promise. But if you go through with this horrible duel and do bodily harm to Jesse Wiley, I assure you that I shall never speak to you again!"

With that, she wheeled and ran away from him. She stopped in the shadows by the carriage house, waiting for him to follow. She supposed the poor man would come running to beg her forgiveness and to promise whatever she might wish.

Hash Harker stared in amazement at the girl dashing away from him.

"Hell," he grunted to himself.

He didn't want this duel any more than anyone else did. It had been forced on him by circumstances. He didn't want to hurt Jess Wiley. And he certainly didn't want Jess Wiley hurting him. He wished now that he'd never spoken up in behalf of Miss Lucinda's honor. He wished he'd never written off and promised to marry her. Especially now that Junie Wiley was free of Dominic.

"Hell," he said again. Some days it seemed like nothing worked out right.

"It'll all work out all right," January told Weston Finlay. She hefted the Colt revolver she had taken from the carriage house. It was Jess's gun, and she'd fired it before. She knew its range and peculiarities. "Likely it won't take me more'n one or two shots."

Weston nodded. He felt a little sick.

"You fetch him on down to the creek," she said.

He nodded again.

She gave his hand a quick squeeze, then hurried off to hide herself in the brush.

Weston found Harker standing alone, frowning pensively. As he approached his victim, he rehearsed his speech. Arriving, he looked up into Harker's face and said, "I — uh — er — I . . . you — uh . . ."

"Huh?" Harker responded.

"Talk to you — uh — alone . . . by the creek."

Whatever it was, it seemed to have the little man highly agitated. Harker decided to go along and see if he could offer some comfort. After all, it was a good host's duty to put the concerns of his guests above his own.

At the edge of the water trickle, Weston stopped and spoke again. "Here . . . wait . . . be back in a minute . . . you wait."

With that, he dashed off.

A gunshot.

Likely some of the men were celebrating, Harker thought.

Another shot.

It sounded close by. He hoped nobody got hurt. It would take the edge off the party.

A third shot.

He thought of the duel again. He hoped nobody got hurt in that either. Especially not him.

A fourth shot.

Crouching behind the scrawny trunk of a young cottonwood, Weston Finlay watched and winced at each shot. He wished desperately that January would get the range and get this thing over with.

January squinted down the barrel of the revolver, carefully taking aim. She was sure she was dead on the target, Hash Harker's left calf. She'd been just as sure with each other shot, but she was doing as badly as if there weren't a single bullet in the gun. She wondered if she might be losing her eye. Maybe she ought to find time to get more practice.

She squeezed the trigger again.

Hash Harker glanced around. That much shooting in celebration ought to have some shouting along with it, he thought.

Another shot.

And Harker was still standing there unscathed.

January bit down on a silent curse. She almost flung the empty gun away. But that would get it all dirty, and Jess would have to clean it, and he'd know someone had been using it.

"Sir?" Harker called with an edge of impatience. Whatever could have happened to the nervous little stranger in the derby? "Sir?"

No answer.

Harker shrugged, turned, and headed back to the party. Once he was out of sight, January emerged from the brush. She'd seen Weston hide. She found him hunkered behind the cottonwood, his eyes clenched shut.

"Mr. Finlay," she said. "You all right?"

"Is it over?" he asked.

"Uh-huh."

"Is there . . . there much blood?"

"I missed him. Every danged time, I missed him. Now it's too late."

Weston looked up at her. Sympathetically he said, "Oh, Miss January, I'm so sorry!"

"Me too! Well, I guess I'd better get back and put Jesse's gun back 'fore he misses it." She held a hand out to Weston. "Come on, we'll think of something else."

Jess wished he could think of something else, but no matter what he set his mind on, it kept going back to the duel. He sure wasn't looking forward to standing up and getting shot at.

"Jesse!" Dominic shouted at him.

He recognized the pottery jug Dominic was waving toward him. Suddenly he felt powerful dry. He shoved through the crowd around the bar. Dominic had poured for him by the time he got there.

"Special," Dominic said, holding out the glass full of mescal. "For you. And for Hash. Nobody else."

"How come?" Jess asked as he accepted it.

"On account of the duel, I reckon. Junie brought it for you."

212

Jess downed the drink. The mescal was as strong as a bull and as sweet as honey. He wiped his mouth with the back of his hand, then said, "She's one hell of a fine sister."

"I reckon," Dominic grunted. "Another?"

"Sure." Jess held out the glass. He could feel the warmth of the mescal reaching into his mind. It was beginning to numb his worries.

He emptied the glass a second time, and told himself maybe everything would work out all right after all.

CHAPTER 18

Jess let himself be cajoled into joining a square on the dance field. He smiled and nodded at folk and tried to look like he was enjoying himself as he went through the motions in time to the music, but his heart just wasn't in it. He didn't even know the girl he was partnered with, and he didn't care.

He'd just lost her in a grand-right-and-left and was wondering if he'd recognize her when they met around the circle, when an eerie wail startled the night.

The music halted abruptly. So did the dancers. Folk looked at each other in question. At least half of them frowned and asked, "What was that?"

Among the other half, a goodly portion frowned and said incredulously, "A locomotive?"

The rest frowned and said, "Damned if I know."

Jess saw the vulture rise from the carriage-house roof and flap out across the *llano* toward the source of the strange sound. He lost sight of it. But then he caught sight of something on the horizon. In the moonlight it looked almost, but not quite, like a small herd of cattle. It seemed to be proceeding with terrible slowness toward Hardly.

The wail repeated itself.

July, her gun in her hand, pointed and hollered, "Look!"

The thing on the *llano,* whatever it was, was drawing nearer. Lights had become visible in it. A sudden burst of sparks shot up from it.

The wail came again.

Men ran for horses. Women ran for the young children they'd left bedded on the floor of the Harker kitchen. Older children ran for sticks and stones and any other handy weapons, then raced toward the lights. Mothers screamed for them to come back. Men on horses passed them. More men on horses, and some afoot, disappeared in the other direction.

Jess had unsaddled the gray before he turned it out. He stopped in the carriage house long enough to grab his rifle from the saddle boot. He didn't bother to hunt up his handgun or saddle his mount. He didn't even bother to hunt up his own horse. He grabbed the nearest animal at hand.

The long-legged bay tied in one of the carriage-house stalls was a Virginia-bred hunter that Hash Harker had paid prime money for. Jerking loose the tie, Jess threaded the rope through the halter rings and the bay's mouth. He swung himself up onto its bare back and slapped his spurs at its sides. The astonished animal leaped into a gallop.

Several riders had started before Jess. He passed them. Soon he was far enough ahead to be wishing he had bet a few dollars on himself before he left.

He could see the lights clearly now. Most of them were lanterns. Above them hung a brilliant disk like a second moon. It cast a sharp knife of light ahead of it. Horns glinted in the beam. Glassy eyes glittered. Polished brass gleamed.

Sounds accompanied the lights. Hoofbeats. A squeaky, whistly, whispering noise like a tea-kettle reaching a boil. A clanking of chains. A screeching of axles under a heavy load. More noises that Jess couldn't even guess at.

He realized that it was a huge team of oxen, double-yoked eight abreast, that crept slowly toward him. And the vast hulking load they hauled was, indeed, a locomotive.

Men from Harker's party were catching up with Jess now. Ranking themselves on either side of him, they stared at the oncoming spectacle and spoke to each other in hoarse whispers.

The locomotive gave another long wail of its whistle.

Horses shied, bucking and bolting. Jess struggled to keep the bay in hand. He barely succeeded.

The locomotive, an American model designed by John La Fayette Whetstone and built by Niles and Company of Cincinnati, Ohio, prior to the War of the Rebellion, was a masterpiece of steam-engine artistry. Despite its age, it had the bearing and majesty of born royalty. Its brass, worn mellow over decades of loving buffing, gleamed like gold in the lantern glow. Its huge whale-oil headlamp, with the wick trimmed and the reflector polished, stabbed its brilliant beam over the backs of the work cattle. Its firebox, now filled with living flame, gave vitality to the water that was the blood of its boiler. It strained and sang with the terrible energy of its steam, spitting puffs of sparks and clouds of smoke through the baffles of its balloon stack. At the fond touch of a hand on the cord, its bright brass whistle screamed its strength and glory at the night.

Within the cab, tugging the cord, stood a man of bearing as regal as, and of dimensions even more awesome than, the locomotive. Leaning out, he grinned broadly at the spectators.

The men of Hardly shouted recognition.

"It's Big Jim Boohm!"

The locomotive answered them with a bellow of its whistle that sent several more horses into wall-eyed fits.

High overhead, the vulture stared down in rapt fascination.

The engine was not traveling under its own power or on its own wheels. It and its tender rode atop a monstrous flatbed wagon that had been built especially for the purpose. An assortment of chocks and chains held the wheels firmly in place. As far as getting anywhere was con-

cerned, the fire and steam were, at present, su-
perfluous. The fire had been laid and the head of
steam built at Big Jim's order, for one purpose —
so he could blow the whistle as he approached
Hardly.

He gave the cord another tug, spooking a few
more horses, then stepped out of the cab and
made his way along the running board to the pi-
lot. He posed there in the spill of the headlamp.

Doffing his cap, he made a small bow to the
assemblage. He addressed them in a voice that
filled the night.

"Gentlemen, I have returned!"

A cheer went up from the men of Hardly, the
bull drivers, and the others of Big Jim's entou-
rage. The fireman tossed more wood into the
flames, and the stack spewed out a gust of
sparks.

Whisk Shaker, who'd grabbed himself a mule
and had only just caught up to the crowd,
pushed forward and called to Big Jim. "Does this
here thing mean that the railroad's finally coming to Hardly?"

"Hasn't one come yet?" Big Jim said.

Men shook their heads. Some sighed mournfully.

"Give it time, gentlemen. Give it time," Big
Jim said. Then, before anyone else could speak
up, he changed the subject.

"I am presently on my way, gentlemen, to
Alaska. I have made a long and strenuous detour
in order to honor the people of Hardly with the

218

opportunity of seeing the *New Belle of the Arctic.*"
He waved a hand, indicating the locomotive.
"And to invite those of you who have the daring
and the foresight to do so, to join me in the
greatest enterprise of this, or any other, cen-
tury!"

"What enterprise?" a somewhat sour voice
called.

Big Jim spread his hands for silence. It was a
grand gesture that seemed to encompass his listeners, one and all, and to draw them spiritually
toward him. He spoke softly now, his words
given as in confidence to each man as an individual.

"In all fairness, gentlemen, I shall withhold
my announcement until I am addressing the entire citizenry of Hardly. I wish to share this glori-
ous opportunity equally with one and all
together. I assure you it is an opportunity big
enough, magnificent enough, for the whole
world!"

With that, he bowed again and returned to the
cab of the locomotive to give another blast of the
whistle.

Some of the mounted men fell in to escort the
train. Others spurred up their horses and hurried
back to spread the news. At the word of the spectacle that rolled toward them, most of the folk
who had stayed behind picked up and hiked out
to meet it.

It arrived in front of Hash Harker's house surrounded by cheering men, women, and chil-

dren, some afoot, some astride, and some hitching rides on the massive wagon, the engine, and tender, and the oxen. As it rolled to a halt, the musicians rushed ahead to their stage and prepared to give Big Jim Boohm a proper welcome.

Big Jim pulled the whistle cord once more, then gave orders for the fire to be extinguished, and climbed down from the cab.

The band answered the locomotive with a prolonged fanfare of drum-thudding, banjo-tremoloing, flourishes on the guitar and fiddle, a wailing of the concertina, whining from the Jew's harps, and deep umph-umphing from the bass jug.

The people crowded around Big Jim as he strode toward the bandstand. They cheered and hollered for a speech. He had expected no less from them. He climbed up onto the stage, lifted his hands for attention, and beamed benevolently at them.

They gawked expectantly back at him.

Big Jim Boohm was a man well deserving of his appellation. In his high-heeled boots, he stood over six-foot-five, and he was fleshed out like a good beef steer. His brown eyes were bright and piercing, his teeth were as beautiful as Ali Ibn's (one bicuspid was solid gold), and his flowing muttonchop whiskers were a deep rich brown touched with dignified gray. He was built bigger, could talk louder, walked taller, and cast a longer shadow than most men. And he knew it.

Poised on the stage with his arms outstretched, he might have been some heroic statue, bigger than life, representing the grand nobility of man's dreams and destiny.

"I bring you the fulfillment of your dreams and destiny," he proclaimed, his voice rolling across the audience like the chords of a massive pipe organ. "I bring you opportunity more golden than you have ever before conceived. Cornucopia tilts her golden horn above your heads. You have only to reach out if you would grasp the riches she is prepared to bestow upon you!"

"You bringing the railroad in, Mr. Big Jim?" Pecos Pike called hopefully from the crowd.

"More than that," Big Jim replied. "My friends, listen, and I will tell you of an enterprise that will span the globe, linking the Old World with the New, and bringing untold prosperity to those wise enough to anticipate it."

Murmurings among the crowd ceased. In silence, the entire audience gazed at Big Jim.

He told them, "At the northwest corner of our beloved continent, in the American Territory of Alaska, there is a point of land which is separated from the great continent of Asia, and thereby Europe, by no more than a narrow gap of water known as the Bering Strait!"

He paused while his listeners whispered among themselves in wonder at this revelation.

After a moment, he gestured for silence again. "As you undoubtedly know, there are plans

221

afoot for the construction of a railway from Moscow, in Russia, across the vast steppes of Siberia."

People glanced at each other. If anyone among them had known about it, he'd kept it to himself.

Big Jim continued, "As yet, there has been no official announcement of the terminus of this line. However, it is most certain, in fact only natural, that the line should extend to the furthermost point of land on the coast of Asia — that point of land on the Bering Strait which is so close to our own Alaska. And what more logical than that the Grand Canada-Mexico Railway should be extended to reach the Bering Strait, and that a bridge should be constructed across that trickle of water which will link the two mighty continents of America and Asia — that will, indeed, span the globe!"

Again the people glanced at each other. To a man, they agreed it was most logical.

"Now, of course it will be necessary for there to be a port of entry at either end of this bridge," he told them. "A great commercial center through which goods and passengers will flow. A city which will outrank the leading seaports of the world. And we — the adventurous spirits who aren't afraid to reach out and take success by the tail — you and I, together, shall journey to the Territory of Alaska, where we shall stake our claims and prepare the city that will accommodate the tremendous commerce of the linked continents. We will be the founding fathers, the

first citizens, the leaders of this magnificent enterprise!"

The crowd cheered.

Big Jim shushed them. Leaning forward, he
said confidentially, "You know, folks, the way to
get ahead in the getting-rich business is to be on
the spot *before* a railhead arrives."

Several members of the audience muttered to
themselves unintelligibly.

Big Jim gestured grandly toward the locomotive. His voice thundering again, he said, "As a
token of my own deep abiding faith in this mon-
umental enterprise, I am bringing along with me
the *New Belle of the Arctic.* This magnificent
steam engine shall be the first, the veritable flag-
ship of the vast fleet of railroad trains that will
shuttle between the continents, making obsolete
the slow and cumbersome and actually danger-
ous seaships presently handling the Orient
trade."

"The Orient!" Dominic Johanssen shouted.
He could contain his enthusiasm no longer. He
plunged through the crowd, leaped to the cab of
the engine, and grabbed the whistle cord. With
all his weight and joy, he pulled.

The last of the steam left in the cooling boiler
escaped the whistle in a piteous squeal. And
then the cord broke.

On stage, Big Jim beamed at the gathering. He
spread his arms and told them, "Now, friends,
on with your celebration!"

CHAPTER 19

Almost everyone who'd come to the partying had brought along bedding of some sort or other. Even at this time of the year, nights could get kind of chilly on the *llano*. A few folk had actually bothered to unroll their bedding in sheltered corners and under wagons. Some had gone so far as to bed down inside their wagons. Most lay scattered around among the debris of the partying, curled into tight little knots against the night cool.

Jess, at the corner of the horse corral next to the carriage house, had fetched his saddle blanket. He was wrapped tight in it when the first hint of dawn wakened him.

The spot he'd picked to bed in was sandy, and a little squirming had shaped it to fit his body. It was every bit as comfortable as the lumpy hay-stuffed mattress on his bunk at home. He should have slept well and wakened feeling fit, but he didn't.

He came awake slowly, with the stiffness of tension aching in his muscles and a fuzzy stuffiness in his head. Shrugging his way out of the saddle blanket, he shivered, sat up, rubbed his eyes, and remembered the duel.

"Hell," he said aloud.

Something stirred at the sound of his voice. He squinted at the moving shadow atop the smokestack of the *New Belle of the Arctic*. It was the vulture. Evidently it had roosted there for the night.

Sure, Jess thought, it wouldn't want to miss the duel this morning.

The sun was still behind the horizon, and the dim dawn glow had no warmth in it yet. Pale mists lay in the hollows under the trees that lined the creek. There was a fresh green smell of damp vegetation in the air. Jess breathed deeply of it, hoping it would clear some of the fuzziness out of his head.

This was the best time of day for traveling, he thought. It'd be real pleasant to mount up and cover land before the sun got high enough to heat the rocks hot enough for frying on them without a fire. Ride in the dawn and the dusk, sleep during the dark and the midday.

Yeah.

He supposed he ought to chouse up Jacob and Whisk and find out what was happening.

The partying ground was covered with vaguely discernible lumps that were folk asleep. Searching through them, he inadvertently woke Dominic and several others. Dominic joined him. The others mostly grumbled or cursed and went back to sleep.

A while of searching convinced them that Jacob and Whisk weren't among the people sleeping around the stableyard, so they extended their hunt, heading toward the creek.

The mists that hung over the water were beginning to rise. They'd be gone completely by the time the sun cleared the horizon. The leaves of the willows that were damp now with mist would be crackling dry. Day came harshly in the *llano*. But for the moment there was a cool moistness and a soft serenity. It seemed almost shameful for a man to be moving about, intruding on the idyllic peace.

A sound intruded on the idyllic peace. An intermittent rasping noise.

Stopping Dom with a touch of his hand, Jess whispered, "That's Jacob."

"Huh?" Dom said.

"That's Jacob," Jess repeated. "I'd know that snore anywhere."

Dom cocked his head and listened. A thin wheezing accompanied the rasp of the snores.

"He ain't alone," Dom said.

Jess sighed and said, "Well, I got to see him and find out what's going on."

Dom nodded, and they proceeded toward the creek.

It turned out to be Whisk Shaker who wheezed the soft accompaniment to Jacob's snores. The two were lying side by side on the bank of the creek, their boots in the water.

First Jess tried speaking to them. Neither stirred. He tried splashing water in Jacob's face. That didn't work. He lifted Jacob's head and shook it. A contented smile spread on Jacob's mouth, but his limp eyelids didn't so much as flutter.

"Hell," Jess said.

Dominic held up something he'd found in the brush. It was a cut-glass decanter. Empty. He said, "They been at some kind of fancy drinking-liquor."

"Act more like they'd been into Ma's laudanum," Jess muttered.

"What's this?" a big voice boomed from behind him. "What seems to be the matter, friends?"

Jess let Jacob's head flop. Turning, he looked up. Big Jim Boohm stood there in his shirt sleeves, with his vest and coat over one arm. His collar button was loose, but his hair had been brushed and slicked down. He smelled faintly of lilac water.

Sorting out the vest and slipping it on, Big Jim asked again, "What's the matter?"

Dominic bowed slightly. Dreams glistened like stars in his eyes as he spoke. "Mr. Boohm, I'm going with you! All the way! To Alaska, and then, when the bridge is built, all the way to the Orient! I always wanted to go to the Orient. I'm gonna take the Palace with me. It packs up flat for shipping, you know. I'm gonna have a genuine Oriental saloon!"

Clapping a huge hand on Dominic's shoulder, Big Jim said, "That's just fine!"

Dominic beamed.

Big Jim shook out the coat, then slid an arm into a sleeve. He got the other sleeve on and started to fasten buttons. Frowning down at Jacob and Whisk, he said, "But what seems to be the problem here?"

"It's supposed to be a duel," Dominic said. He launched himself enthusiastically into the whole story.

Big Jim listened with studious interest. When he had heard Dominic out, he turned to Jess. "Can't this matter be settled without bloodshed?"

"I don't reckon so. Hash seemed right set on that point."

"And neither second can be wakened?"

Jess nudged Jacob with a boot toe. There was no response. He shook his head.

With an air of true nobility and sincere regret, Big Jim said, "Then I can see no recourse but to accept the duty that fate has thrust upon me. I shall act as your second in this affair myself."

Joy radiated from Dominic's face. "You hear that, Jesse! Mr. Big Jim Boohm, the Builder, himself, is gonna stand up with you!"

A small but resounding cheer sounded.

Wheeling, Jess discovered the spectators. A dozen or so folk had wakened and drifted over to see what was happening.

The cheer roused people still sleeping around the partying ground. Rumpled, bedraggled, bleary-eyed, and unkempt, but eager not to miss a thing, they rolled out of bedrolls and clattered out of wagons. Some still barefoot, some who'd slept in their boots, some dragging along squawling children, they hurried to the bank of the creek to listen and watch.

Big Jim Boohm beamed at them.

With somewhat less enthusiasm than Dominic felt the occasion warranted, Jess said, "I'm obliged to you, Mr. Boohm."

"Call me 'Big Jim,' son."

Another cheer went up, this one fuller and more robust than the previous one. The crowd of spectators had at least trebled in size, and more people were joining it every moment.

Pecos Pike Griswald, with his galluses pulled up over his bare shoulders and his shirt in his hand, asked, "What about a second for Hash Harker?"

Puffing up, Dominic said, "I reckon I'd better stand for Hash after all."

"No," Big Jim answered. He remembered his collar button. He fumbled with it as he said, "I must be absolutely fair and impartial in this matter. Therefore, I shall act as second for both gentlemen."

Dominic's proud joy fizzled into bewilderment. "But . . . I . . . Hash . . . Can you do that?"

"Is there any reason I shouldn't?"

"I mean, the rules . . . if I had the book I'd look it up, only I give the book to Hash for Jacob to read."

"Jacob can't read," Jess said.

"I mean, Hash was gonna read it to him."

Big Jim asked, "Where is Mr. Harker?"

July came squirming out of the crowd. "Likely still over to his house," she hollered. "I'll fetch him."

She dashed off with Hassan close behind her.

"Sprightly child," Big Jim muttered. He looked around. Just about everybody who'd come to the partying was up and watching. He asked, "The duel is scheduled for this morning?"

Nods and affirmative mutters answered him.

"And the ground?"

Dominic said, "Wherever you pick out, Mr. Boohm."

Pursing his lips, Big Jim considered. He nodded at his own decision. The creek ran almost straight along here. Clumps of brush, outbursts of grass, and small stands of willows lined it. The land was generally level, and back from the bank of the creek, was only sparsely sprinkled with low growths of vegetation. The spectators were gathered mostly on one side.

"Over there," he said, gesturing toward the open area on the far side of the creek. "That should serve quite well. Will a medical man and a man of the cloth be in attendance?"

"Matt Matthews?" Dominic called out. "Reverend Seven?"

"Here!" The Reverend P. Jonathan Seven called as he came scuttling toward Big Jim.

"Pomegranate!" Ezekiel W. Trot shouted at him.

Automatically, he responded with a cry of, "Apple!"

Dominic grunted in disgust.

"Apple?" Big Jim Boohm asked.

"Them two is always at that," Dominic told him. "Ain't never but they're fighting over was it an apple or a pomegranate Eve et in the Garden of Eden."

"Is that so?"

"It was an apple," the Reverend said smugly.

Ezekiel W. Trot shouted, "Was a pomegranate!"

"Mr. Boohm," Dominic said. "You're a man of traveling and learning and things like that. Maybe you could settle this here thing once and for all. Do you know which it was?"

Big Jim Boohm gestured for Ezekiel W. Trot to come forth from the multitude and stand beside the Reverend. He studied the two of them thoughtfully.

"Now, as I recall, it says in the Good Book that when Adam and Eve ate of the fruit of the tree, their eyes were opened and they knew that they were, ah, naked," he said.

Ezekiel W. Trot and the Reverend both nodded.

" 'And they sewed fig leaves together and made themselves aprons,' " Big Jim quoted at them.

They nodded again.

"Well, it seems to me that if a man and a woman suddenly discover themselves to be improperly attired, they will make use of the material closest at hand to cover themselves. Would that not seem so?" Big Jim looked out at the gathered crowd. He got a response of nods and murmurs. No one disagreed.

"Is that not so?" he asked specifically of Ezekiel W. Trot and the Reverend P. Jonathan Seven.

They both nodded.

"Then, I would say that the fruit our honored ancestors ate of," Big Jim proclaimed, "was the fruit of the fig tree."

"Fig?" Ezekiel W. Trot said.

"Fig?" the Reverend P. Jonathan Seven echoed.

"Fig," Big Jim Boohm repeated authoritatively.

Ezekiel W. Trot and the Reverend P. Jonathan Seven looked at each other abashedly. In unison, they said, "Fig?"

"Here comes Hash!" someone on the outside of the crowd shouted.

July led the way. Head high, backbone stiff, Harker followed her. He had dressed himself in his best black broadcloth suit with the conservatively matching vest. He had a frilly white ruffle down the front of his shirt, lace at his cuffs, and soft yellow gloves on his hands. A flat chest of mahogany was tucked under his arm.

Women ooohed at the sight of him.

Doffing his wide-brimmed planter's hat, he made a bit of a bow. " 'Morning, Big Jim. Dom. Jess. Folks."

Heads bobbed in reply.

Hash looked down at the supine, snoring forms of Jacob and Whisk. "It's true, then, what July tells me."

"Our seconds up and blunked out, and now we can't rouse them," Jess said.

"Fear not," Big Jim said. He went on to explain that, if Harker had no objection, he would be acting on behalf of both principals.

"I got no objections," Hash answered. "I'd be downright honored."

"Ah, *honor*," Big Jim said with a mellow smile. He repeated the word, savoring it, then turned to face the spectators.

The sun was sitting fat and round on the horizon now, and it gave a golden glow to the gathered crowd. The last of the mists were gone off the creek, and so were the dregs of sleepiness for all but the youngest children. Babes in arms nursed contentedly. Toddlers sucked at pacifiers of cold ham rind. A young mother finally managed to shush both of her squawling twins. Complete silence descended. Excited faces and eager eyes held rapt on Big Jim Boohm.

He let them wait a moment longer, knowing the thrill of anticipation they felt. Then he began to speak.

"It is a matter of honor that brings us here to this noble and perhaps tragic field today. Honor between gentlemen. The honor of womanfolk. Indeed, it is honor as well as the steel rail and the iron horse, and the vision of the people, that has made our nation great. It is the sense of honor that distinguishes civilized man from the lowly savage. Friends, a man can find no nobler nor more satisfying death than in defense of honor. 'Mine honor is my life; both grow in one; take honor from me and my life is done.' Richard the Third."

For one instant longer there was silence. And then a cheer broke forth. A rousing, roaring, thunderous cheer that rolled out across the *llano* and sent the startled vulture soaring with an angry squawk from its perch on the smokestack of the *New Belle of the Arctic*.

Big Jim bowed graciously in acknowledgment of the accolade. Then he turned to Hash Harker again.

"I understand you refuse to accept less than spilled blood in satisfaction of this matter?"

Put that way, it seemed to Hash that the only honorable answer he could give was, "Yes."

"Weapons?" Big Jim asked.

"Me and Hassan'll fetch their six-guns," July said eagerly.

"No, child," Big Jim told her. "A matter such as this is not to be settled with common six-guns. The code of honor prescribes matched single-shot, smoothbore pistols."

"Huh!" July looked aghast. She winced as Hassan prodded her, and met his dark questioning eyes with appalled uncertainty.

"Got them here," Hash said. He opened the mahogany chest. Nestled in fitted compartments lined with satin were two stiff-necked brass-bound pistols with long damascened barrels and finely carved walnut butts.

"Magnificent," Big Jim said.

July and Hassan squeezed in for a closer look.

Hash grinned with pride. "They were Grandpa Cleeland's. Harvey Nugle and William J. Phippstide both tasted lead from these when they crossed Grandpa."

July tugged at Big Jim's sleeve. "But they *got* to use their own six-guns."

"The code is quite specific," he told her.

Jess told her, "Shut up."

"Jesse, please —"

"You shouldn't even ought to be here."

"But, Jesse!"

"July, please, for me, will you just shut up and stay out of the way?"

Reluctantly she stepped back. She blinked and wiped at her nose as she watched. Hassan put a gentle hand on her shoulder.

Big Jim asked, "You gentlemen both ready?"

Jess and Hash both nodded.

"Where is the medical man?"

"I'm here!" Matt Matthews hollered. He hurried forward, waving the large carpetbag that contained his surgical tools.

"I'd appreciate your help with the preparations, doctor," Big Jim said. "Would you be so kind as to mark off the ground? I'd say about thirty paces."

"Sure enough!" Matthews grinned. He dug a

score into the earth with his heel and began to step off the distance.

"And you, sir." Big Jim turned to Dominic. "Would you please see to it that all the spectators are safe on the far side of the branch?"

"Yes, sir!" Dominic answered, delighted to be of service. He waved at the audience and began shouting, shooing the strays back across the creek.

Turning away from them all, Big Jim strolled up-slope a ways. With his back to the crowd, he squatted and opened the gun chest.

With respectful gentleness, he lifted out one pistol. He opened the powder pan, forced back the hammer with the heel of his hand, and dry-fired the gun. The hammer spring was stiff and heavy. The pistol jumped in his hand like a goosed mule. Feeling severe doubts for its accuracy, Big Jim set it down and tried the other one. That was no better. Fair enough, he supposed. He up-muzzled one and began to pour powder into its barrel.

July watched fretfully. With his back to her that way, she couldn't see what Big Jim was doing, and Dominic wouldn't let her across the creek for a closer look. He couldn't stop her from drinking, though. She hunkered at the water's edge and scooped up a handful. From there, pretending to drink, she could look between Big Jim's thick legs.

She saw his hands tilting one pistol, pouring powder into the muzzle, following it with a wad, then ramming the wadding carefully into place.

As he set down the first pistol and started on the second, July grinned to herself.

When he'd finished, Big Jim replaced the pistols in the fitted case and strolled back downslope. He held the open case out toward Jess.

"As the challenged party, Mr. Wiley," he said, "you have first choice."

Jess plucked the nearest pistol from its nest. It was a heavy hunk of iron that felt unnatural in his hand.

Hash Harker took the remaining gun. He held it as if it were a poor fit for his fist.

"To the scores, gentlemen," Big Jim said, stepping back.

CHAPTER 20

The long bright light of the rising sun stretched across the *llano*, giving a crisp, sharp definition to every shadow. The partying ground, with its scattering of litter, overturned trestle tables, and empty bedrolls, had an aspect of a deserted battlefield. Not a thing stirred upon it. In the corral, horses nickered and called for a forking of hay, but they were ignored. Everyone who'd come to the partying was at the bank of the creek now.

The masses of people gathered, in their party finery, rosy and golden in the dawn, like converts at a river of baptism. But their finery was rumpled, their hair tousled, and though their eyes were bright, many faces were still puffy from the sudden interruption of sleep. Their murmuring lacked the pious solemnity appropriate to a religious rite. An aura of electric excitement hovered over them. It reflected in the taut tones of their comments one to another.

Two men remained oblivious of the occasion. Jacob Wiley and Whisk Shaker still lay still, their boots in the creek, their faces in contented smiles, their snores mingling with the mutterings of the crowd.

Dominic's shouts cut sharply through the

morning. He sounded like a cowhand rousing the beef critters off a bedground as he raced around the gathered crowd, herding it back, all to one bank of the creek. Yielding to him, people elbowed and jostled, grunted and cursed, as they tried to get the best watching positions. Dominic added curses of his own at the stragglers who refused to fall into properly ordered ranks according to his instructions.

Across the creek, on the bare ground beyond the scant brush and drooping willows, Jess Wiley and Hash Harker took their positions on the scores that Matt Matthews had scratched on the ground. Each held a pistol heavily at his side. Big Jim Boohm, the barber-surgeon, and the minister had moved upslope, well away from the principals.

Jess and Hash glanced at each other, then looked at Big Jim. The spectators looked at Big Jim. The murmuring ceased. Dominic stopped his herding to take his own position. He held his breath. Only soft snores interrupted total silence.

Big Jim said, "Ready, gentlemen?"

"Ready," Hash said.

"Ready," Jess said.

"I shall count to three," Big Jim told them.

Hash nodded.

Jess nodded.

The crowd waited.

"One," Big Jim said.

Jacob lay on his back. Sunlight touched his

eyelids. Sounds and a vague suggestion of thought intruded into his dreams. He had a notion there was something important he had to do — something he should be doing at this very moment. He rolled over and started to rise.

Big Jim called, "Two."

Jess's finger was snug on the trigger of the gun at his side. His eyes were steady on Hash. He had the line of fire, the lift of the pistol, set in his mind. His body was ready to act.

"Three."

As Jess swung up the pistol, his eyes snapped shut. That hadn't happened to him since he was just a tad first learning to fire a gun. Blindly, he squeezed the trigger.

The pistol bucked. The trigger pinched his forefinger. Two blasts rolled together into a single roar that slammed into his ears. Behind the clenched eyelids, he felt the sting of powdersmoke.

He forced open his eyes. Through a heavy haze, he saw a figure leaning forward, slowly falling.

It wasn't Harker.

Somehow someone had come onto the field at the instant of fire.

"Jacob!" Miss Lucinda screamed.

Jess flung away the empty gun. Sucking at his pinched finger, he ran toward the fallen figure.

Miss Lucinda was there before him, on her knees at Jacob's side. She cradled Jacob's head in her hands. Jess knelt next to her. Then Matt

Matthews was there, and Ali Ibn as well. And Hash Harker. And Junie, clinging to Harker's arm, staring aghast at Jacob.

"Oh, God," Harker said faintly.

The crowd closed in.

"Stand back! Stand back!" Dominic was shouting. He ran up and down, waving his arms as if he were shooing chickens. "Stay on your own side of the creek! Stay, I say!"

Jacob moaned.

Big Jim stepped forward.

"He's all right. Just give him room," he said. The mighty thunder of his voice rolled back the crowd, opening space around Jacob and Miss Lucinda, Junie and Hash and Jess, the barber-surgeon and the hakim.

July crept to Jess's side. She asked, "He ain't really hurt, is he?"

Jacob opened his eyes. They looked fuzzy. He grinned abstractedly.

"No, little lady," Big Jim told July. "He's not hurt."

July winked at him. For an instant he seemed taken aback. Then he returned her wink.

He turned to Hash. "Is your contention satisfied now?"

Jess pulled the pinched finger from his mouth and held it up. The skin was broken. A droplet of red oozed out. He said, "I've spilt blood, if that'll satisfy you."

Hash nodded. "If Miss Lucinda is satisfied, I sure am."

He glanced at Miss Lucinda, hoping she wouldn't want him to carry this any further. But she was too rapt in clutching Jacob's head to her bosom to take notice.

At the edge of the crowd, January pulled her hand from Weston Finlay's. Against Dominic's protests, she crossed the creek and ran to Jess's side.

"He's all right, sis," Jess said, looking up at her.

"Are you?" she asked.

He nodded.

"Jesse, take care." Her voice was soft, very warm, and gentle. She leaned toward him and gave him a sudden kiss on the cheek. Then, blushing, she wheeled away. She dashed back across the creek to grab Weston by the hand and drag him out of sight behind the crowd.

"Huh?" Jess stared after her.

"I think I'd better clean these," Big Jim Boohm muttered as he bent to pick up one of the abandoned pistols.

"I'll help you," July offered.

"Me too," Hassan said.

Matt Matthews and Ali Ibn had been conferring over Jacob. They nodded in agreement, and Ali Ibn stepped out to face the crowd.

"Ladies and gentlemen, it delights me to inform one and all that this gentleman, Jacob Wiley, was not so much as touched by a bullet," he announced. "He is simply in a trance, a laudanum stupor."

The crowd cheered.

Dominic mumbled to himself, "Nobody was hit at all."

Jess and Hash shook hands.

Hunkering at Big Jim's side, July watched him swab out the bore of one pistol. She giggled and nudged Hassan.

"I don't get it," he told her.

"You can load all the powder and wadding you want," she said. "But it don't mean much if you don't put no pistol ball in with it."

"Young lady," Big Jim said with mock sternness, "you have a very vivid imagination."

"And right keen eyesight," she answered him.

He harrumphed and continued cleaning the pistol. After a moment he winked at her.

The show was over. The crowd had begun to break up. Womenfolk were collecting their children and the pots and pans they had fetched foods in. Menfolk were catching horses and saddling or harnessing up. The vulture had returned to its perch on the carriage-house roof. And the Reverend P. Jonathan Seven and Ezekiel W. Trot were walking off slowly, side by side.

"Fig," the Reverend said dolefully.

Ezekiel W. Trot gave a sad nod. Then suddenly he brightened and said, "Well, if it hadn't been a fig tree, it would have been a pomegranate."

Perking up, the Reverend answered, "It would

243

have been an apple."

"Pomegranate."

"Apple."

Together, they drifted on.

Jess sucked at his pinched finger as he walked back to his mother. She was still sitting where he'd left her, in her rocker with her eyes closed and a contented smile on her face. In the rocker next to her, Mrs. Delphinia Quick, with her boots off and her laces loosed, was snoring softly.

Jess touched his mother's shoulder. "Ma?"

Mrs. Deke's eyelids didn't flicker. Her lips barely moved. "Jesse?"

"It's time to go home, Ma."

"Where's Mr. Wiley?" she asked.

Jess glanced around. He saw the buzzard on the carriage-house roof. Its wings were folded, and its eyes were on him. He wondered if he should point it out to his Ma.

She saw it for herself. She smiled and said, "There he is. You reckon he enjoyed the partying?"

"I reckon," Jess answered, thinking the buzzard wasn't the only one who'd enjoyed it. Jody had just appeared in the doorway of the carriage house.

The boy paused long enough to see to it that all his buttons were buttoned and his belt was buckled. He tottered out into the morning sun, scrubbing his fingers through his hair. Nance followed a few steps behind him. Catching up, she nudged him and guided him toward his mother and brother.

" 'Morning, Jesse," she said with a soft little smile.

" 'Morning," he said.

She leaned against Jody's side. The boy's eyes were hazy, his smile distant. He seemed to look right through Jess without ever seeing him.

Nance said, "Wasn't there supposed to be the duel this morning, Jesse?"

"Uh-huh."

"What happened?"

"Nothing much. Nobody got hurt."

"That's nice," Mrs. Deke said.

Jody focused fuzzily on his brother. "Duel? You done had it already? That's funny, I didn't hear no shots."

Jess glanced from the boy to the girl and back again. "Funny, huh?"

"Jesse! Ma! Jody! Everybody!" July shouted from the distance. She was bounding toward them, with Hassan close at her heels.

"What?" Jess hollered back at her.

She skidded to a halt in front of him and answered, "It's January. She's done run off with that little Mr. Weston Finlay feller!"

"What!"

"Uh-huh! Soon as she found out you wasn't getting killed in the duel or nothing, her and him up and run off. They told Junie what they meant to do, and she gave them Dominic's rig and filly as a getting-married present, and they went and set out for the county seat!"

"That's nice," Mrs. Deke said.

"You reckon we ought to go after them?" July said. "I wouldn't mind shooting that Mr. Weston Finlay feller if you'll give me some bullets."

"Hell, no," Jess said. He touched his fingertips to the spot on his cheek where January had kissed him.

"What you gonna do about them, Jesse?" Jody asked.

"Nothing. Leave them do what they want. Everybody ought to get the chance to do what he wants least once in his life," Jess said.

Jody nodded profound agreement.

Nance tugged at Jody's sleeve. Rising on tiptoe, she whispered into his ear. His face reddened. He nodded and slid an arm around her shoulder.

"Mrs. Deke," the girl said tentatively, "I — uh — you're gonna need a woman around the house, and July ain't old enough to take on all them chores."

"Nor willing," July mumbled, cocking a brow at her.

"I was thinking, Mrs. Deke, I always wanted me a home and folk to take care of. If I was to come live with you, I could . . . you . . . I . . ."

"She's coming home with us," Jody said, squeezing her with the arm he had around her. He looked defiant, as if he intended to fight anyone who denied him.

Jess looked at him critically. "You reckon you two could take care of Ma, huh?"

"Uh-huh."

"And you really want to?"

"Uh-huh."

"All right. You harness up the wagon and take her home. And you take good care of her, you hear?"

Without waiting for an answer, Jess wheeled and strode away.

"What you reckon's got into him?" Nance said.

Jody shrugged. "Don't matter none. He can take care of himself."

"There's things he's been putting off too long already," Mrs. Deke murmured.

"I'll fetch the wagon," Jody said.

Mrs. Deke asked, "Is it time to go?"

"Yes'm."

She nodded slightly toward the woman asleep in the next rocker. "The widder Quick's coming home with us. Gonna visit with us for a while."

"That's nice, Ma," Jody said.

Holding an almost empty laudanum bottle gently against her middle, Mrs. Delphinia Quick (widowed), formerly of Fairwater, Virginia, smiled contentedly in her sleep.

Back by the creek, Miss Lucinda Cummins of Fairwater, Virginia, still clutched Jacob's head. And Junie Wiley still clung to Hash Harker.

"Junie," Hash said softly. He gazed into her face.

She returned the look expectantly. "Hash," she said.

Miss Lucinda looked up at Hash just as he turned to look down at her. Both spoke in the same instant.

"Mr. Harker, I'm afraid there's something I have to discuss with you," she said.

"Miss Lucinda, I'm afraid there's something I have to discuss with you," he said, his words marching in step with hers.

They met in a moment of silent understanding. Miss Lucinda nodded. Hash smiled. Miss Lucinda returned her attention to Jacob. Hash turned back to Junie.

July and Hassan followed Jess to the corral. They watched in silence as he saddled the gray. It wasn't until he stepped on board that July spoke to him.

"You ain't going back home now, are you?"

He shook his head.

"Where you going?"

"Don't know yet."

"Coming back?"

"Maybe," he said. "Someday."

"Why don't you go to Alaska with Mr. Boohm?" she asked.

He glanced up at the buzzard perched on the carriage-house roof. "Maybe I'll go down to Mexico, see what I can find out about Pa."

"If you find out, will you come back?"

"Maybe. For a while."

"But not forever?"

He shook his head and touched his spurs lightly to the gray's sides. It started to amble away.

"Jesse," July called after him.

He halted and looked back.

"You better load up your gun again," she said. "You ain't got nothing but wax for bullets."

"On account of the duel?"

She nodded shyly.

"And Hash's got the same?"

She nodded again.

"Sis," he said. It sounded as if he'd meant to say more. But he didn't. Instead, he dug into his saddle pocket. He brought out the cartridge box he'd picked up at the Gen. Mdse.

"Here." He tossed it toward her.

She caught it. "For me?"

"All for you." He gigged the gray again, setting it into a gallop.

"A whole box of cartridges!" Hassan said, awed. "Can I shoot off some? Can I?"

July glanced at Jess again. He was well away, traveling fast now. She opened the box and held it toward Hassan. It was full of pebbles.

"You got them already?"

"Yeah," she said. "But it's the thought that counts."

From the carriage-house roof, the vulture had seen the two-wheeled rig rolling off with Weston Finlay at the reins and January Wiley at his side. It saw Junie and Hash head toward the house, leaving Miss Lucinda and Jacob by the creek. It watched Jess ride into the distance. Then it saw the wagon with Mrs. Deke and Mrs. Delphinia in the back, Jody and Nance in the front, head toward the Wiley place. It glanced down at July and Hassan as they collected the pinto and rode into the *llano*.

Spreading its wings, it rose into the morning sky, circled once, and flew on.

The employees of G.K. Hall hope you have enjoyed this Large Print book. All our Large Print titles are designed for easy reading, and all our books are made to last. Other G.K. Hall books are available at your library, through selected book-stores, or directly from us.

For information about titles, please call:

(800) 223-1244
   or
(800) 223-6121

To share your comments, please write:

Publisher
G.K. Hall & Co.
P.O. Box 159
Thorndike, ME 04986